FSC
www.fsc.org

MIX

Papier aus ver-
antwortungsvollen
Quellen
Paper from
responsible sources

FSC® C105338

Book Cover Design by RockingBookCovers.com

Story 2019 ©Copyright by Hiam Mondini

Translation by Patricia Magdalena Redlin

Proofread by Nicholas Modlin

Printed and published by BoD – Books on Demand, Norderstedt

ISBN: 9783750407749

"Stolen Lives - Part II"

Hiam Mondini

written on a BlackBerry Classic again

(no, I don't get sponsored… yet!)

For Chuck

INTRODUCTION

"No, no, no, no, NOOOO!!!! Not again! You've got to be kidding! You're going to lose your job yet again, my love! What the hell am I calling you "love" for? You're a stupid, unreliable and irresponsible space case! Nothing more, nothing less! Seriously, woman! C'mon, get the lead out!!" All this time she has been yelling her head off at herself, Rosalía has thrown her duvet to the floor, taken off her nightgown and stepped into the shower, absolutely furious with herself. "Oh yeah, sure, hallelujah! Of course, this has to happen today! Stupid shower! Ungrateful landlord! What a start to my day!"

Enraged, the small Mexican woman climbs back out of the green tub as ice-cold water drips from the rusty faucet. She grabs a fresh towel from the shelf unit in the corner and buries her still dry face in it. She takes a deep breath, inhaling the fresh scent – lavender from

5

Provençe – and for just a fraction of a second it seems like that beautiful picture of a lavender field on the fabric softener bottle is not just an empty promise. "Okay, then just a cold sponge bath and I'll take a shower after my noon workout. And you should stop talking to yourself, Rosa, it will be the end of you..." She fills the small sink with cold water, sprays a bit of cologne into it and dips the lavender-scented washcloth into the refreshing water, then immediately dabs it onto her face to soothe her skin. She catches her weary expression in the mirror and sighs softly, "You will age very, very quickly this way. Who knows, maybe today that cute guy with the baby will come back, and you will definitely not make a good impression looking like this! I wonder if he is a single dad... "

Chapter 1

She can feel her heart pounding in her throat. How is it possible that a single organ can cause the body so much discomfort? One organ, as big or small as your own fist, controls everything. No heart – no human, it's so simple. Heart broken – sad human. Heart pounding – excited human. Heart beating wildly – angry human. What kind of person would you get if all three of these hearts made music together? Broken, pounding and beating? Linda would say this is exactly what she is right now. And just to add a bit more spice to the situation, she mentally mixes in a pinch of injury, grief and reeking anger. There, done! She chews nervously on her cuticles and is surprised to catch her reflection in the mirror. So, it's actually true that they put these mirrors in police interrogation rooms! She gets up and walks slowly towards it. In the movies, they always show someone standing on the other side of it, observing the people. Is anyone observing her right now? But why should anyone be interested in what she is doing? Also, this is not an interrogation situation, so there's really nothing to see here. Just a nail-biting wreck of a woman with ridiculously little patience.

What's taking so long anyway? She looks in the mirror again and observes herself. How could this have happened, Jasmine? What is happening? Roberto! She suddenly screams his name loudly at the mirror as if he were standing behind it. "ROBERTOOOOO!!!! WHYYYY???" She breaks down sobbing and crouches on her knees on the floor just as the door flies open and Frank rushes in. He hurries over to Linda, kneels down beside her and takes her in his arms, hugging her tightly, stroking her dark hair lovingly and kissing her head to comfort her, "Shhh… it's alright, I'm back. Everything will be okay, Linda. Everything will be okay… Shhh." He presses her tighter to his chest and feels her trembling. He gently helps her up and stands with her, gently rocking her in his embrace. "She´s here, Linda. We'll get some answers to our questions soon. She´s here..."

Linda abruptly stops sobbing and releases herself from Frank's embrace. "She is HERE?! At this station?! Here?! Where?! Where is she?! I want to see her! Where is Roberto?! Is he here, too?!" Like a startled, disoriented animal, she stares wide-eyed at her faithful companion. She tries to go to the door, but he grabs her hand firmly to hold her back.

"Just wait, Linda, she'll be right here. I know, every second is difficult to endure. Just be brave, my love, and hold on just a little bit longer. She'll be here soon. Then we'll grab the bull by the horns. I promise you! We're almost there!"

He takes her tear-streaked face into his big hands and, as he has done so often in the past few weeks, he wipes her swollen eyes dry with his thumbs and softly caresses her flushed cheeks.

"I'm so proud of you! You're doing great!" Just as he is speaking these comforting words, the door opens.

Chapter 2

In the stifling, humid air of the Mexican town, even the locals' brows are covered in transparent beads of sweat. It's precisely because of this heat that all the usual hustle and bustle has slowed to a leisurely pace. There's no rushing, no honking, no loud chattering. Today, as always, Rosalía seems to want to go against the grain. Running across the street in her new, golden sandals, frayed denim shorts and a white lace top, she greets the bus driver with a radiant smile.

"Hola Pedro! Espérame!" she says, and jumps onto the ledge of bus, which has just been brought to a halt by the city's oldest bus driver. The ancient Hispanic grins at the gasping woman through a bushy mustache, as he does every morning, displaying the gap in his teeth. "Buenos días, Señorita! Pretty shoes, but quick, we have to go. I can't be late every day because of a pretty Señorita..." Rosalía winks at the man, who is always so nice to her, and blows him a kiss as she walks past him. "Muchas gracias, mi amor! How is your foot? Is it still swollen? Will you let me check it again?" She sits down in the front seat so that she can see the driver well and make eye contact in his large rear-view mirror from time to time.

Almost 30 minutes later, Rosa has had her coffee, devoured a banana and checked her email. Again, no positive answer. Pedro, as if reading her disappointed thoughts, makes a hissing sound to get her attention in his big rear-view mirror. "Díme belleza, what are your plans for your trip abroad? When are you going to abandon old Pedro and break his heart?" He grins mischievously through his beard, once again exposing his dental problems. Rosalía puckers her lips into a kiss towards the mirror of the bus and winks, "How am I supposed to go anywhere without you? You and your bus are coming with me, have I not told you that? Doesn't matter where I'm going, mi amor! But unfortunately, the universe apparently has mucho, mucho, mucho more patience than I do." She rolls her eyes, takes a deep breath and looks out the dusty window. Pedro keeps looking at her in the mirror, wondering when his dreams died. When did he stop reaching for stars? Would he die behind this wheel?

"Hasta luego, Pedro! Drive carefully and come over soon! Promise?" Rosa spryly leaps out of the bus and blows another kiss over her shoulder to her favorite bus driver as she flings her old leather handbag over her shoulder. She begins to run.

"If you really step on it, you can get your timecard stamped in time. Don´t talk now, run!" Her daily workouts appear to be paying off and she makes it there on time. Out of breath, with her arms on her hips and slightly dizzy, she puts one foot in front of the other, holding the stamped timecard in her hand, and makes her way to the staff dressing room. She opens the door, which now seems to weigh a ton, drags herself slowly over to her locker and sits down on the wooden bench in front of it. She takes off her brand-new sandals, which are definitely not suitable for running, pulls her top over her head and is about to get up to remove her shorts, when the door opens and Carmelita enters.

"Hola! I thought you weren't coming in today! So, what's going on? What have you been up to? Oh wow, have you been working out? Is that a six-pack I see?" She chews excitedly on a piece of bubble gum, which Rosalía has never liked. She looks at Carmelita, puzzled, while she buttons up her white smock and responds politely. "Good morning to you, too! Yup, I just made it. Why would I have been up to something? And by the way, I don't think you're allowed to chew gum at the nurse's station..." She grins at Carmelita, ties her long dark hair into a bun and closes her locker door. The other girl sits down on the wooden bench, shoots her a curious glance, and replies, "Well, because the director has been looking for you everywhere!"

Chapter 3

Linda looks with disappointment, surprise and suspicion at this face that she knows so well. His arms are spread widely so she once again removes herself from Frank's embrace. Walking slowly, she approaches the three people who have just entered the interrogation room and stops just short of their now outstretched arms. Before any sound can pass Linda´s lips, she hears a soft sob. "Jasmine, I'm so sorry... My God, Jasmine... If I'd known you... Jasmine, you're alive! You're alive! Jasmine, I can hardly believe I'm seeing you! But what about..." Sensing a gaze wandering down her body, Linda instinctively crosses her arms in front of her flat chest, asking in a cold, almost suspicious voice, "Who told you I would be here? Where's my baby? Where is Roberto?" She takes a threatening step forward and is immediately held back by Frank.

***

"We need to inform all the airports in New York, immediately, as well as all airports in neighboring states. We also have to broadcast the wanted picture and set up the live stream. Jasmine Steiner should appear on screen together with Conley. Having him appear will increase the number of viewers and interest. Come on, get moving! These crooks will not get away!" The FBI agent hisses his words at his crew, his voice clear and purposeful. His audience turns on their heels and leaves to go do the work they have just been assigned. Their team leader walks through the door behind him and stands, legs wide apart with his hands in his pockets, behind the large glass window. This gives him an unobstructed view of the room in which Jasmine Steiner, Conley and their visitors are sitting at a table. Watching Jasmine's facial features, her posture and gestures with his trained eyes, it is clear to him how much despair, fear, confusion and bitter disappointment are swirling inside her petite body right now. She stares at the people sitting across from her like an eagle focused on its prey. Her posture is tense, as if she is about to pounce. Conley notices this too and holds her gently by her arm and shoulders.

***

"Jasmine, please listen to me! I don´t know where they are! I just know that you're alive and that we mourned our loss of you in Switzerland!" Claudia is beginning to sob harder and she can barely get her words out. Torr, her husband, puts his hand reassuringly on her shoulder and takes over for her, saying, "Roberto asked Claudia to empty your apartment because he did not want to come back with Mirjam because you..." His explanation is abruptly interrupted by a loud cry.

Linda grabs her stomach with both hands, as if to crush it, and cries out again, "Mirjam?! MIRJAM!!! My girl! Where is my girl?!!!!" Her entire body trembles and it looks as though she can barely breathe. Frank immediately jumps up, gives the "stop" sign they agreed on in the direction of the mirror and speaks in a polite but very firm tone to the couple across from him, who appear to be frozen. "Time for a break!" He points to the door, which has just been opened from the outside by FBI Agent Mayer. "Please, she needs more time, this is enough for now." Claudia and Torr exit the room, both somewhat confused, leaving a sobbing Linda behind with Frank, who is now hugging her, stroking her back, kissing her head reassuringly and gently rocking her in his arms, "We'll find your Mirjam, and I'm sure she's well and as beautiful and brave as her mother!" At these words, Linda loses control completely, howling into his chest with what little her lungs can still produce. "I thought they got Leslie... I thought Leslie was here... She knows where Roberto and Mirjam are... Frank, I want my baby! Why is Roberto doing such a horrible thing to me?"

Chapter 4

Rosalía walks slowly down the sterile corridor towards the fire escape, with a queasy feeling in her stomach. Maybe that's because the director wants to see her, or it's just that her stomach is empty. She tries to ignore the nausea and hops lightly up the steps. Ever since she has given free rein to her urge to move, moving wherever and whenever possible and letting her heart dance, she is doing much better. Even if the day starts out badly in the morning – like today – she catches herself incredibly fast before she can start to brood, and it's become rare for her to wallow in misery. They told her, warned her even, that it would turn into an addiction. Yes, she has tasted blood and now wants more of it! How could something that feels so good be bad? There's simply no way she will allow the director to ruin her cheerful disposition today. Try as she might, she cannot imagine what he could want from her. She has just passed her probationary period with flying colors and signed and returned her permanent employment contract a long time ago. She hasn't made any mistakes, except for the two... ok, maybe three times when she's been late to work. But to compensate she has accepted extra work every time it has been requested and she has never noted her overtime hours. So he will definitely not have anything to say about her work hours! No, she has washed her hands of any guilt and one of those hands will shake his with her head raised high!

In the management department reception area, the young Mexican woman in white presses the button to announce her presence and the orange waiting button flashes immediately. She sits down on an elegant sofa and it occurs to her where the money that is being cut from her paycheck is flowing. Why is there a sofa in the waiting room in front of the director's office? Do people have to wait here so long that they might need a nap, or is this the old furniture from the director's home? Rosa giggles at the thought as she scans everything in the room. From the paintings on the walls to the heavy rug underneath the lounge table, everything makes it look like a cozy living room rather than a psychiatric clinic. Maybe they hold some of the therapeutic sessions here so the patients finally get to feel well. Once again, Rosalía smiles at her own sarcastic thoughts, then notices the green blinking button that looks like it's about to explode. "Yes, I'm coming...!" She smoothes her pressed scrubs, wipes her forehead, takes a deep breath and opens the door confidently.

"Señorita Dominguez! Come in! Or was it Señora?" The director is short and balding and wears thick glasses. He takes Rosalia's hand in greeting and puts his left hand on top of it. It's a gesture that she has never liked because it feels oppressive and controlling to her. She squeezes briefly, then frees her hand from the director's overpowering grip, offering a polite smile in return, and takes a seat. "Rosalía is fine. You wanted to speak to me, Señor Director García?" She folds her hands in her lap as if to pray and looks at him curiously with her big brown eyes.

"Yes, I´ve been told that you don't waste any time! You do a great job here with us and it makes me very proud to have you on my team, Rosalía. I have also heard that you are exceptionally trustworthy and reliable! These are traits that I really need right now!"

The delicate physiotherapist's curious gaze slowly morphs into an expression of confusion and bewilderment. She leans her head slightly to the side and looks at him questioningly. "So what exactly is this about?"

Chapter 5

"That dry beanstalk! If I get my old sausage hands on her, I'll make firewood out of her! But what am I saying? Oh boy, that rattling stick probably wouldn't even start a fire. She would disintegrate like a match! No, she should suffer. I should go to the library! I need torture books from the Middle Ages. There's bound to be something useful in those!" Susie, the typically kind-hearted receptionist from Coney Island Hospital in New York, is pacing back and forth at the police station like an absent-minded professor with a crimson face. Claudia and her husband Torr are sitting on a bench nearby, both with sad and desperate expressions on their faces. They are lost in thought, sipping from cups of cold watery coffee. A young policewoman walks briskly over to Susie Manders, touches her gently on a shoulder, so as not to abruptly yank hour out of her loud and angry bubble. "Ma'am, excuse me please, ma'am?" Susie looks at the young woman with narrowed eyes and hisses, "What?" "You're scaring people..." The policewoman gestures demonstratively in the direction of the police station, where at least forty eyes are staring at Susie with expressions of amazement, horror, indignation and fear.

"Well, you should probably arrest me right now because if I catch this Leslie, I guarantee you I will do something illegal! I promise you this here and now before all of these gawking witnesses!" She makes a dismissive gesture in the direction of the gawking witnesses and looks at the Coney Island Guard policewoman with confidence: "Ok, ok, honey, don't worry, you don't need to be scared. This old, chattering goose here is not dangerous... Not yet... Well anyway, I'm calm now... Where are Frank and Linda?" Susie scans the room as if she has just come to pick someone up.

"I can't, or actually, I am not allowed to tell you that, ma'am," replies the policewoman, somewhat perplexed, and she grabs her holster with both hands. "Manders, my dear, this ma'am is named Manders! I'm not a fan of 'ma'am', if you don't mind?" Susie spreads her hands like a three-way mirror around her round hips. "Not at all, Miss Manders, but I can't give you any information. If you are not a relative, then..." She is interrupted by Susie's loud cackling. "Not a relative, you say? Who do you think you have in front of you? Now hurry up and tell them that Mama is here. Hurry, hurry!" She tries to dismiss the officer by waving her hands around, unsuccessfully. "And whose 'Mama' are you?" the officer asks, her facial expression now both annoyed and amused.

"Susan Manders? Is there a Susan Manders here?" An FBI agent steps into the open space, reading the name aloud from a card in his hands.

"Here I am, my savior! Sherlock Holmes over here was about to try to solve a murder mystery!" As she blurts out these words, she winks at the astonished policewoman and then whispers at her in passing, "Don't be so serious, my love, that frown will only give you wrinkles and make you ugly. But if an elderly lady says she's the mama, then she *is* the mama. Doesn't matter whose. But she's part of the clan. You understand?" Countless television series have taught her that it would be extremely awkward to pat an armed official on the back, so she clicks her tongue and struts in the direction of the FBI agent with her head held high. "Hello, sir, where are we going? I hope you do not have to handcuff me?"

Chapter 6

Lost in thought, Rosalía strolls down the stairs, sliding her fingers down the banister railing. Memories of her mother´s words flood her thoughts. "Don't, my love, you never know who might have touched that or how dirty their hands were. There must be thousands of bacteria on it." The Mexican woman, still distracted, immediately lifts her hand off the bacteria source and puts her thumb and forefinger around the pendant hanging from her gold necklace. She sits down on the stairs and says aloud, "I miss you, Mima. If only I could tell you... But soon ... Very soon I will write exciting stories that will make you happy. Your little love is doing well, doing wonderfully well... or at least I will be soon, very soon! And you will have the best treatments and the latest technologies so you will be able to hear the voice of your little love sing again. I just got an exciting job. Just imagine, of all people, he chose me... "

"That sounds like a very exciting plan!"

Rosalía leaps up in shock, turns around and looks into the most beautiful green eyes she has ever seen. "You have an accent!" Rosalía stutters into the tall man's beaming face. He approaches her and leans casually against the source of bacteria, a necklace flashing through the opening of his shirt collar. The nervous physiotherapist wonders if the necklace was a gift, too – perhaps from the mother of the baby?

"You're one to talk! You sit here talking to yourself excitedly and then you make fun of my accent?" He smiles, his gleaming, perfectly straight white teeth now complementing his mischievous green eyes.

"I wasn't making fun, merely expressing my surprise. I... I... Have nothing against accents – all over the world, except here in this country, I also have an accent." Embarrassed, Rosalía tries to escape from this extremely unpleasant situation and turns towards the stairs.

"Surely you won't just leave me hanging like that, will you? What kind of plan are you hatching? Need an accomplice?" The gorgeous Adonis with his accent casually crosses his arms in front of his chest, flexing it and causing Rosalía to feel even more embarrassed and look away.

"I'd rather work alone and, to be honest, you make me nervous! That's not good for me, I need a clear head today. Not just today, of course, I always do. But especially today. You see? You can't just interrupt me when I'm talking to myself and then ask so many questions and show me your white teeth and your muscles and... And I have to go to work now. I have, I will, I should... Mi amigo!... Hasta luego!"

***

For the fourth time this morning, Rosalía is out of breath and standing by the coffee machine in the staff room, holding onto the table like it's a life raft. Now, some coffee... That should help her to clear her head again.

"I told you, Rosa. Talking to yourself like that will be the end of you. It has to stop. You've got an important job to do. You can't screw it up." She presses the button for a Café Americano and watches the watery brew pour slowly into a disposable cup with the clinic´s logo printed on it. She purses her lips, then notices a white reflection moving in the reflective surface of the chrome-plated machine. Focusing on the bright spot, her eyes grow gradually bigger before she slowly turns around.

"I'm not doing it on purpose! I'm really not!" He waves his hands in front of her face in self-defense. Those magical green eyes are lit up again.

"You can't be here. This is the staff room! Only people who work for the clinic are allowed to be in here to talk to themselves." Embarrassed again, Rosalía buries her hands deep in the pockets of her white smock and turns to the rattling coffee maker, closing her eyes, biting her lips, hoping that the machine doesn't reflect the color red. When she realizes that the bright spot is not moving away from the machine, she takes a deep breath and says, "No accomplice, and that's final!"

From behind her back, Rosalía hears a faint whistle, followed by the sound of someone clearing their throat, "Hmm, I wonder if I should tell the Señor Director about this?" Now curious, but without turning around, Rosalía asks, "The Señor Director?"

"The Señor Director. He assigned me to you. So if you can turn around, without talking to yourself or being nervous around me, I'm happy to introduce you to your new intern!"

Chapter 7

"Camera is running!" The cameraman points a finger at Frank, for whom this gesture is a matter of course, in the same way that the midwife is a matter of course for passed out fathers in the delivery room. He looks into Linda's sad eyes, takes her hand and kisses it in front of the camera. The gesture seems to surprise not just the entire crew, the FBI and the Coney Island Police Department team, but also the owner of the hand, who looks at Frank with a puzzled expression on her face. The world-famous action hero winks at her lovingly and smiles at her reassuringly. "Ladies and gentlemen, dear friends and helpers, may I introduce you to the most brave, courageous and determined woman I have ever encountered in my life. My name is Frank Conley and this is Jasmine Steiner. We have an extraordinary request for you!" The skilled actor points his index finger directly at the camera, looking extremely somber. "Jasmine has had terrible things inflicted on her. The most painful of all is that her child has been taken from her in a horrible way. Please help us and call your local police station or the number shown below if you have seen either of these people in the last two days." The cameraman points his finger at a man behind a laptop, who immediately blends in two photos of a woman and a man onto the monitor. Linda's soft sobbing is now audible and she looks at the camera in despair, eyes pleading and voice hoarse, "Please, please, help me find my baby..."

***

"Ah, just seeing this picture of the skinny, white-haired snake is enough to make my donut collar burst! Come to me, Linda, my sweetheart, Mama wants to hug you now. Never trust a rattlesnake. I should really trust my gut feeling more. Yeah, yeah, don't look at me like that, even under all this insulation, my gut still has wonderful sensors that work flawlessly. Mama Susie should just listen to them more! Now let me hug you, Linda, my love!" This kind-hearted receptionist, once a stranger, pulls Linda's arm to draw her in and presses her tightly to her ample bosom, swaying two or three times quickly back and forth, holding the miserable woman by both shoulders. Susie looks lovingly into her swollen eyes, "This is not a good look for you, it's not pretty. You should smile and look forward to the fact that we will have Mirjam with us soon. Our messiah here has spoken, and with all these women in our country who are watching television, who can't wait to report someone to the police and get a personal thank you from their superhero, we'll have her back in a flash. I'm telling you, the wires are hot now. Believe me, sugar puff, if this takes more than 24 hours, Susie will personally eat a vegan pizza. I'm going to take you home now. That's enough for now, right, TV boy?" Susie turns to Frank, who is engrossed in a conversation with the FBI agent, but immediately senses that he's being spoken to. "Yes, that's great, you two go ahead, I'm still talking to Van Thiels." He approaches the two women, puts his hand on Linda's shoulder and bends down to her. "Is that okay with you? Lou is waiting downstairs, and so is Tom, who will keep the nosy reporters off your back."

"Oh, how exciting, can I keep them off my back myself?" Ever the happy soul, Susie pokes gently with her elbow and winks mischievously at Frank, who is rolling his eyes.

"Do what you have to do, but don´t take any of them to my house!" He is just about to show them to the door when Linda turns to him, saying, "I'm sorry about the way I behaved with Claudia. Do you think they can visit us tomorrow? I think I could handle seeing them tomorrow. One night, I just need one night, to dream about Mirjam..." She wipes away another tear, wraps an arm around Susie's to leave, and tries to force a smile. "Here we go, Miss Manders, to the Paparazzi party!"

As soon as the door has closed behind the two women, Agent Mayer waves his hand to

Frank and his colleagues in excitement. He's holding a telephone in his other hand and nods euphorically. "And you are absolutely sure, sir, that this is the woman in the picture? No doubts at all? She looks the same? Ok, ok, very good, please stay where you are! Don´t go after her! Yes, I know that and that is a possibility, but there is already a team on the way as we speak. Please do not approach her. It's important that she doesn't know she is being watched... I know that, too, sir... No, please, no, stay where you are! Try to be inconspicuous... Sir?... Sir?... Hello??? Damn hero wannabe! I hope he doesn't mess this up for us!"

Chapter 8

Somewhat tense and with a pounding heart, Rosalía, pretending to be cool, walks with her new intern down the sterile corridor to the patient lounge. Of course, she would fall for an intern! Why couldn't he be some lanky guy with a center part, thick horn-rimmed glasses, bad teeth and an acne-scarred face? She barely finishes the thought, and she can already hear the gentle voice of her mother, "My love, do not judge a man based on his external characteristics. Even if a person doesn't look perfect to you because of developmental difficulties, birth defects, or just bad luck, everyone can have a wonderful soul and a loving heart. Those two virtues are far more important in our lives than outward appearances." Of course, a wave of guilt fills Rosalía's stomach and she calls herself a fool to have such thoughts.

"Señorita? Rosalía?" A deep, soft male voice penetrates her musings and she feels a hand gently touching her shoulder. She looks into the intern's dreamy green eyes, shaking her head a little, saying, "I can't keep doing this! When and where do I get to talk to myself if you're following me everywhere? Then I'll go insane from having to silence my conversations with myself, and I will ultimately be declared incompetent!" To her surprise and utter astonishment, his green eyes wink at her and he brings his perfect face in closer to hers while calmly citing, "'When two people are walking together, they will notice each other,' Homer said, once a poet of the Occident." A deep sigh is the only response Rosalía knows how to give. Of course he would also be well-read, cosmopolitan and good at quoting! She gives up, surrenders to her fate and remembers her upcoming, intensive workout at noon.

"Do you play sports? No, wait, stop, of course you do, OBVIOUSLY, so wrong question. What sports do you play?" Rosalía purses her lips, her eyes narrowed into mischievous slits, and waits for him to answer. Her intern puts both hands into the pockets of his white smock, raises an inquisitive eyebrow and answers, amused, "I'm up for anything!" He snorts and clears his throat with one hand over his mouth. "I'm sorry, that slipped out! I meant that I love all sports. I'm really not picky. The main thing is that I can keep this body fit. After all, you only get one body in life, right?" Curiously, he looks down at the little woman and leans against the doorframe.

"Could you please, please STOP that?!" She gestures wildly at the arm supporting his weight and walks away thinking to herself, "So, up for anything, huh?! Well, then I will certainly meet up with him in the gym!" She waves a disdainful hand over her head and heads out through the door.

"You know I can hear you?"

"No me importa!" she whispers softly through her rose-colored lips and smiles to herself.

"Okay, just making sure! I'm curious and feeling as tense as a Swiss crossbow, to find out what this gym is all about, and what you do there!"

Rosalía stops in her tracks and turns to face her Adonis intern. She focuses on his green eyes, still heavenly green eyes, and asks in surprise, "Swiss crossbow?"

Chapter 9

Bonnie, the goodhearted manager of the Conley House, brings out tea, a plate of fresh pastries, a full fruit bowl and a carafe filled with water, lemon wedges and peppermint leaves from the garden. Susie winks at her over her sunglasses and shakes her head, "Tell me,

Bonnie, how is it that you're so perfect? Everything always smells good, looks immaculate and you, yes, you always look the same, like you´re on a film set!" The housekeeper smiles, embarrassed, and sets the table in the luxurious garden patio with purposeful hand movements.

"Leave it, Bonnie, I'll do it!" Linda rises from a cozy, pillow-covered corner seat and takes the red-haired woman's napkins out of her hands.

"Linda, you know Frank would not like that. You should get some rest."

"Yes, yes, I know. But I don't need any more relaxation, otherwise I'll get worse! I'm doing fine and I need to do something meaningful. Even if it's just setting the table, making my own bed and washing and ironing my clothes, which I did not even buy myself.

43

SURELY you understand me, Bonnie, otherwise you wouldn't do that for Frank every day, would you?" She folds the napkins skillfully and lays them elegantly on the table. "See, I can do that very well! "

"No one doubts that, but hey Bonnie, if the Swiss lady here does not want it, I'd be more than happy to be pampered by you! Tell me, does he pay you well, the Conley lad? Let's say I could get you a slightly better deal, would you stop by and visit me?" Susie's hearty grunt and mischievous expression make all three women laugh out loud.

"Well, what kind of party have we got going here that I was not invited to?" Frank's son Kenneth walks out of the house, dressed casually in shorts and a T-shirt, and heads straight over to the chuckling women. He hugs

Bonnie, kisses her on the cheek and stretches out his hand to Susie.

"Young man, if you're offering hugs, I want some, too!" Susie tries to get herself up out of the deep sofa, which is made a little harder by the fullness of her body, and then declines in mild disappointment: "Well, some other time then, my muscles just do not want to get up, you understand!" She takes the hand he offers her and shakes it as a greeting.

"My father would never forgive me if I denied any woman her wish." The young gentleman gets on his knees in front of the well-loved, slightly rotund receptionist and squeezes her heartily, "Hello, Susan!" Her face turns red. She returns the hug and gives him two light pats on the shoulders: "You're such a good boy! If only my two klutzes had a touch of that elegance … "

After this heartfelt greeting, which they both enjoyed, Ken sits next to Linda, hugs her sideways with one arm and kisses her on the cheek. "Hello, Linda. Tell me, how did it go today? It seems none of you had any cell phone coverage at the station, so NO ONE has informed me! I had to find out from Tom that you were on your way home. So, what's new?" He reaches for the glass of water Bonnie has put in front of him, sips it and turns from Linda to Susie.

***

"I understand, that must have been a shock. I'm frustrated that I could not be there. I can't cancel these lectures on such short notice." Linda knowingly puts her hand on his and subtly shakes her head, saying, "I would not want that, Ken. You and Frank have been spending too much time on me, on my chaos! I've recovered

46

and I can take care of myself, now. I'm not sure yet how I'll ever make it up to you for everything. But I know I will, in my own way, as soon as I can." Before she can say more, Susie hisses loudly, turns her world-weary gaze and points her thumb towards Linda while she looks at Ken, saying, "Listen to this smart little professor! Do they actually teach you what true friendship means in that chocolate-filled Swiss place, Linda?" She taps her leg and calls out towards the house, "My Scottish beauty, we need something a little stronger out here!" She hoists herself up from the pillows, muttering softly to herself, "Keep looking... Tsss... Return the favor... Tsss..." She then opens the patio door to the house.

"Who do we have here? Hello, master of the house! When did you sneak up on us? You will not believe what your little Swiss chocolate cake out there just said..." Frank does not let

Susie finish her sentence, but grabs her shoulders with both hands, "We have them, Susie! We have them!" He reaches for her full hips and swings her around once. Their loud cries attract Linda and Ken, who enter the spacious living room looking distraught. With open mouths and big, bewildered eyes, they stand there with their arms hanging down as they watch the spectacle in astonishment.

When Frank stops spinning Susie, who is now feeling a bit wobbly on her legs, and leaves her standing in the room, he runs to Linda, who immediately rebuffs him. "No thanks, no merry-go-round for me!" Frank beams at her and repeats the words he had said to Susie a moment before: "We have them!"

Chapter 10

"Aaaand another 5... 4... 3... Come on, señoritas, you can do it! Think about your bikini bodies! ... Aaaand one more... Count down to one! Muy bien, chicas! Hasta luego, see you next time! I hope to see your trained butts again tomorrow!" The fitness trainer, just as sweaty as everyone else, reaches for her towel and water bottle on the windowsill and walks over to Rosalía, who is lying on the floor. She lies down next to her on her towel, takes off her headset and, breathing heavily, looks at the ceiling. "Oh beautiful! Look at those cobwebs on this rotten ceiling!" She turns her head to her student, who is still gasping for air, kicks her with her leg and smiles. "Spill those beans! Why did you join my class today? Either all the climbing walls are occupied or you're hiding! Let me guess... A guy?!" Nosy Nellie turns onto her side and rests on one hand, looking at Rosalía curiously, biting her lower lip, one eyebrow raised, and makes a purring sound.

"Stop that, you animal! Tell me, have you absolutely lost your mind to teach such a murderous class when I'm in the room? I can't move a muscle anymore and I still have to work!"

"Aiaiaiai, caramba! This is SO not like you! Is he THAT hot? Where is he? Show him to me!" The well-toned sportswoman is already peeking through the small pane of glass where she can look into the adjoining weight room.

"Cut that out!" Rosalía sits down cross-legged and drinks from her water bottle. "This is awkward enough already! You might not believe it, but I've just been assigned the hottest intern that has ever worked with us, and I have to train and monitor HIM especially carefully... Orders from the director himself!" She straightens her back and salutes as if she were a dutiful soldier.

***

"How cool is that? You wanted to get away from here and hey, going to Switzerland is probably the most luxurious thing that could happen to you! They have those expensive watches and the elegant ski resorts... And snow!!! Rosa, imagine! You in a fur coat, riding in a coach through a romantic snowy landscape with your intern sitting next to you...! Wait a minute... Did you say intern? How old is your wonder boy, anyway?" Juanita wraps her towel around her freshly showered body and looks at Rosalía through strands of wet hair. "Are you turning into a cougar now...?"

"Juanita, please! Why are you saying such stupid things? You have too much imagination or you watch too many American movies! Really! I won't be going anywhere for a long time and certainly not with my intern. And by the way, he was finished with puberty a loooong time ago and this is not his first internship... it's not!" Rosalía quickly applies lotion from head to toe with skilled hand movements and then gets dressed just as quickly. Juanita looks at her in admiration while she herself is still busy putting lotion on her first leg. "Hey, you nut job, are you on the run or something?" Rosa sits down on the bench, slips into her golden sandals, unwraps her hair from the towel and slowly combs it out, staring off into space. "Hmm... No... I'm not the one who's on the run..."

Chapter 11

"But I do not understand. Don't we have to go to the police station?" Confused, Linda looks out of the helicopter, which Mike is skillfully flying to the New York airport. Frank shakes his head and explains through his headset, "They are still at the airport. Cooper has already started the investigation and doesn't want to lose time."

"THEY are STILL at the airport? Who are THEY? And where do THEY want to go?" Linda clings to Frank's forearm. He looks at her sympathetically but shrugs his shoulders. "I don't know anything beyond what I just told you, Linda. We'll find out soon, ok? It won't be long. Look, there's the landing site!" He points with one finger in the direction they're flying and pats Linda's hand, which is resting on his forearm. She looks at the landing site, bites her lower lip and closes her eyes. She takes a deep breath and whispers into the microphone, "Hoffentlich isch de Alptraum ändlich fertig! Ich mag nüme… (I just want this nightmare to be over! I can't take it any longer…)."

"I'm sorry. What did you say?" Frank looks at her questioningly, but then he realizes she was not speaking in English nor was she speaking to him or Mike, so he leaves the question hanging in the air.

***

The two passengers quickly exit from the back of the private helicopter and walk as fast as they can to the door that leads into the building. Frank waves to Mike and makes a hand gesture meaning "I will call you." Mike salutes casually, then goes back to his comfort zone in the skies to return to the Hamptons.

Frank opens the big steel door for Linda so she can enter and hurries into the building after her. Tom is expecting them, and Frank confirms to himself once again that he has found the absolute best manager in the entire universe! The two men greet each other warmly by slapping each other on the shoulder, and Tom politely extends his hand to Linda. She takes it briefly but firmly while looking around nervously. Tom knows how eager she is and, without saying a word, he shows her the way. Accompanied by two airport police officers, the three of them hurry down a corridor and through the labyrinth that is the airport, while Tom reports what he has learned, "Well, this Leslie Smith was recognized by a man who happened to be watching the news on his laptop ...."

"Tom, is Mirjam ok? Have you seen her?" asks Linda, interrupting his narrative. He looks puzzled, glancing first to Frank, then back to Linda. Finally he answers, "No, I haven't seen her... And to be honest, I don't even know if she..."

"Miss Steiner, Mr. Conley! May I ask you to please follow me?" FBI Agent Mayer, who has appeared in the corridor in front of them, extends his hand first to Linda, then to Frank, and shows them to a room with a table and chairs. He is just about to close the door in front of Tom when Frank raises his hand to intervene and says, "Please, Tom, I need you with me." The manager grabs his jacket and walks into the room, nodding. He stands next to the door, against the wall. Frank waves him over and says, "It is important that you witness everything. The press will tear us to pieces, but this way you can hold your ground. Do you understand?" Frank's firm tone of voice tells Tom that he is not only very tense, but also deeply affected and desperate to bring the matter to a successful ending.

"I understand, Frank. Don't worry. I've got your back. Of course, you can count on me!"

Linda is just about to snap and she positions herself directly in front of agent Mayer's face, shouting, "WHERE ARE THEY??!!"

Chapter 12

"You're too late!" Rosalía taps the imaginary watch on her right wrist with her index finger and looks straight into the face in front of her. "I can't imagine that you were stuck in traffic in the hospital, so what excuse do you want to serve up today, señor?" She reaches abruptly for the wheelchair and sets the brake abruptly.

"Well? You know Rosa doesn't like to wait!" She nudges the sitting patient and smiles in delight.

"I, I... Followed the wrong light. That's it, I was looking for red and could only find yellow!"

"Ha! Gotcha! You can't see any lights yet! I've already received your file and read it thoroughly, sir. You won't be able to give me the run-around anymore! No, no! I'm the smart one in this joint, comprendes?"

"Sí, yo comprendo muy bien!"

"Listen to that! You're getting better every day! Let's see if your legs are as good as your pronunciation! Did you practice this part diligently as well?" She holds her patient's upper body with skilled ease and helps him onto an adjacent padded table. "No, that's what I have you for!" The patient is now lying down and laughs as he tries to straighten himself with both arms. "I see, this girl has to do everything herself!" Rosa takes his left ankle in her hand, places his knee in her other and slowly lifts his leg at an angle.

***

"You did a great job today! Muy bien, really. We've got this, right?" Rosalía pats her patient happily on the shoulder and looks into his face, which is half wrapped in bandages.

"Dios mio, if only we knew how this happened! But we do know one thing: you have an amazing guardian angel!"

"I don't believe in those anymore... Once upon a time..." His voice sad, he lifts up his arms, "Can I get a hug?" Giggling, Rosalía walks around the table and bends towards him. "Since you asked so nicely!" She grabs the big man under his arms forcefully and maneuvers him into the wheelchair that is waiting for him.

"Well, I have to admit, no woman has ever handled me like this before. I've got to give it to you, you are good at your job! And I'm guessing you're neither big nor strong, right?" He hooks one finger underneath the blindfold and turns his face in the direction of the physio therapist.

"You can probably already see something, you cheater!" She approaches him slowly and puts her face close to his. "Unfortunately not, but I know that you are very close to me right now, that you exercised on your lunch break and had a glass of carrot juice before you came here!" He grins his widest grin and folds his hands in his lap, as if to pray. Embarrassed, Rosalía slowly moves away from him, cups her hand over her mouth and breathes into it, "Unpleasant?"

"No, not at all! I love carrot juice, but as a patient here you don't get such treats." Rosa sticks her hands in her pockets, spreads her feet in a wide stance, and makes a face like a big question mark. "How do you know that I worked out and that I am small or at least not big?"

"First of all, because you smell like you just showered and put on lotion, and secondly, because as you know, I've learned a lot about anatomy myself. That's how I would guess you look based on the size of your shoulders, arms and hands. Also, your voice suits a smaller, petite person with lots of energy and strength!" Rosalía's mouth opens slowly and she's glad he can't see her blushing face right now.

***

"See you tomorrow, Bob! As always, it was a delight! And do your homework diligently, don't just learn Spanish, ok?"

"I promise, Rosa! Do I get a back rub if I do?" Laughing, the patient turns around in his wheelchair and slowly rolls down the hallway away from the PT, staying close to the wall. Rosalía is still standing in the doorway, smiling. She loves this job! What could be better than to be able to help people after such tragedy? And especially in the psychiatric clinic, there are such interesting patients that you wouldn't find anywhere else.

"Bob, Bob, Bob... what an interesting personality you have...or had... a surgery assistant from New York?... At least that's what you think..."

Chapter 13

Frank Conley is not just a talented and experienced actor, but also a man of style and manners. Sitting directly across from him is a very thin, pale and trembling Leslie Smith. Frank looks calmly into the eyes of the person who has been taken into custody and smiles at her pleasantly, "Nice to see you again, Leslie! Actually, it's REALLY nice to see you again!" He emphasizes his words deftly and folds his hands on the table between them. The woman he's talking to does not look at him, but at her hands, which she has folded in her lap. Her thin, blonde hair covers her pale face as well as her trembling shoulders. Frank hears her swallowing, loudly and dryly. He looks up at the surveillance camera and asks, "Could we please get something to drink?" He says to Leslie courteously, "What would you like? Coffee? Tea? Would you prefer water or something with sugar? A Coke?" He lowers his head to catch a glimpse of her face, but it doesn't show any expression. He glances back at the frame on the ceiling and adds: "We would like a little bit of everything if possible, thank you!"

***

"Damnit! Has he lost his mind? What is this? A damn luxury hotel or what? He should get that woman talking instead of crawling up her skinny, criminal ass! It's bad enough that he is allowed to talk to her alone!" The young airport police officer tasked with getting drinks leaves the adjoining room with a look of fury on his face and lets the door bang shut behind him.

Agent Mayer does not take his observant gaze away from his screen – he merely waves his hand in the direction of the door that has just closed, saying, "That little blowhard should be playing air traffic controller on the runway. He has no business being here." Turning to Linda, who is staring calmly but intently at the monitor in front of them, he says, "I'm sorry, airport police aren't always the most sensitive. Frank's doing great in there. He's doing everything just like we discussed beforehand. I'm sure he'll be able to crack that hard nut! Who could resist Frank Conley...?" He realizes immediately that this last question might not be particularly appropriate at this moment, so he folds his hands over his mouth and continues watching the action hero in the next room through the screen on the table in front of him.

***

Frank gets up from his chair and takes it with him as he walks around the table. He places the chair next to but a little farther back from the blonde woman, who still appears unfazed. The action hero takes his seat and rests his forearms on his legs so that his face is lower than Leslie's. He looks down and says in a soft voice, "I know exactly how you feel now, Leslie. From the bottom of my heart, I can honestly sympathize with you and I am so indescribably sorry!" His words surprise not only everyone in the next room – even Leslie slowly raises her head and looks at Frank's reassuring face with sad, swollen eyes.

***

"What did he say? He sympathizes with her?! That's something new!" No one noticed that the little blowhard has come back into the observation area and that he is now standing in the open doorway with a tray full of drinks. Agent Cooper quickly walks over to him, takes the tray from his hands and sends him back out of the room with a firm head movement. "What?... But why?..." Confused, the officer, now empty-handed, steps back into the hallway and stares at the door as it is closed in his face.

"Can I take the drinks in, please?" Linda is now standing in front of Cooper and holds up both hands, expecting to take over the tray. "I've calmed down, honestly, I won't yell at her..." Cooper shoots a questioning glance at Mayer, who shakes his head vigorously. "Absolutely not! He is close to it, look! Ssh... He's whispering something to her! Turn it up!" He nudges the IT specialist sitting in front of the monitor and moves his head closer to the speakers.

Mayer, trying to quote what Conley is saying, "He has also lost?... Or stolen? What did he just say? Dammit!"

Chapter 14

Rosalía hops happily up the stairs in the direction of the dressing room. What an exciting, wonderful day! Juanita's torturous class at noon released so much adrenaline in her body that every single cell was activated for a few hours. Nothing could beat this incomparable, amazing feeling, not even being in love!

"Well, this is how we do things, right, Rosa? Exercise, keep moving, a healthy and balanced diet, a job that fulfills you, great friends and family... who needs a stomach full of butterflies?" she blurts out.

"Oh, I think this tingling feeling in my stomach is just irreplaceable!" Rosalía leaps up the last step, as if stung by a bee, and clings to the banister. She looks down the stairs to find the origin of this declaration. Her heart is still beating in her throat and the vein in her neck is pounding visibly. "SANTA MIERDA!!!! That's enough!!! Are you stalking me know!? You, you... You're a sadist! Yes, that's exactly what you are. You, you want me to be locked in a cell and strapped to a bed! You want to put me in a strait jacket!" Rosalía's outburst echoes loudly and ominously throughout the stairwell. The intern's mischievous smile fades slowly from his face, as does his healthy glow.

***

They are still sitting silently across from each other when a small woman with a baby wrapped in a baby sling tied to her chest, also holding a bouquet of red roses in her hands, stops beside them. She holds the bouquet in front of Rosalía's face and looks inquiringly into the intern's green eyes. He says, "I would very much like to buy a rose as a renewed apology, but only because I assume that you wouldn't accept the whole bouquet, right?" Ashamed and uncomfortable, he looks questioningly at the beautiful Mexican woman, who raises one of her naturally curved eyebrows in suspicion and looks at the flower lady, asking, "Say, how much does a package of diapers for your baby cost?" Her incoherent question gets an immediate and unambiguous answer.

"Well," she says to her Knight of Roses, "although I like roses very much, I prefer to look at them in nature rather than in a vase, so I

69

suggest that you give this working mother enough money to buy a package of diapers and I will forgive you this one last time!" She raises her index finger, waving it threateningly in front of his face in an attempt to underscore this point.

"You got it! Agreed! But, because that makes me very happy and because I know how many diapers a baby needs, I will up the amount to buy another package!" He reaches into his pocket, takes a bunch of bills out of his wallet, counts off four of them and presents them to the woman holding the roses and the baby. "Muchas gracias, Señora, you have saved me!"

The woman thanks him and leaves with the money, the sleeping baby and the roses to sell to the next guests in the cozy garden cafe.

***

Rosalía is cuddled up on her cushioned sofa in her small but very cozy living room. As soon as she has made herself comfortable, she feels her cellphone start vibrating. "I can hear you, but I do not remember where you are! Hasta luego! Rosa just wants to read, enjoy a delicious glass of wine and have no human contact whatsoever. So, whoever is making you vibrate will have to wait for me until tomorrow. How wonderful! There's no one here to interrupt me while I'm talking to myself!" Despite her confident words, Rosalía stands up and looks cautiously around the room. "Nope, no one here. It would have been too much if Mr. Perfect had suddenly come out of the bedroom and interrupted me to give me his two cents' worth!" She turns towards the bedroom, then towards the bathroom, shakes her head a little and rolls her big, dark eyes. "Now I'm getting paranoid... That fits in perfectly with my tendency to talk to myself! Well done,

Rosa!" She sits back down, pats her thigh, takes a sip from her glass, places it on a stack of books that serves as a side table, and opens the book in her hand.

"Why didn't you ask if you want to know so badly? The baby must be his, if he knows how much diapers cost... But where is the baby? And where is its mom? He doesn't wear a ring... Oh, Rosa, you know your assignment is clear, and you are obviously more than curious... Tomorrow! Tomorrow, it's your turn to ask the questions. No more prattling on about exercise plans and nutrition and hearing aids! Tomorrow, I'm going to give that pretty boy hell... Chew him out?... Rake him over the coals? No.... I should read and learn the right words... Maybe from these romance novels... But not today... Today we're traveling to the Scottish Highlands where we will be enchanted... We??... Who's we!!?? Let's put schizophrenia on the list, too!"

She draws an imaginary check mark in the air and dives into her Scottish Highland saga.

Chapter 15

"She honestly does not know..." Frank puts both hands on his hips and paces up and down the corridor, running his fingers through his dense, slightly graying hair and looking with disappointment at his son. "When I finally made her talk, I thought, Now, NOW, we have her! And soon Linda can hold her daughter in her arms and hold her husband to account´... And then, SIMON offers that damned escape plan!" He emphasizes the name with a mixture of malice and disgust. "This whole situation is all so revolting! And this Roberto!! A typical Italian mama's boy! Can´t make up his own mind!" As soon as he finishes his sentence, Ken clears his throat and nods his head in the direction of the corridor behind Frank, who, still boiling with frustration, turns around in astonishment to see Linda standing there with sad eyes, obviously having heard his strong words.

"Linda, I'm sorry, really! But I cannot understand why he would go along with them… That he would fall for it..." Frank says as he shakes out the last of his fury with flailing arms. He approaches Linda and tries to hold her by the shoulders, but she takes a step back and looks at him with disappointment, saying, "I do not want to believe that either! Roberto is not... There must be more behind it... I saw his eyes... I looked him in the eyes when Simon..." Her own eyes fill with tears, which she immediately wipes off on her sleeve, biting her lip.

***

"Please call me Linda! There is no more Jasmine. You took care of that yourself, Leslie!"

Linda sits opposite the stiff blonde woman and looks directly into her deep-set eyes with a resolute gaze.

"I'll leave you to your fate very soon. I just want to know two things and I beg you to give me honest answers. I think I deserve this... Or rather, you owe it to me!" She massages her right hand so hard it starts to chafe. Leslie notices this powerful reserve and nods sheepishly. Linda looks at the camera on the ceiling, then back to Leslie. "When and where did you last see Roberto and Mirjam?"

Leslie, who has also followed Linda's glance at the surveillance camera, turns her attention back towards Linda. She purses her lips as if she needs to contemplate her answer first, then lowers her eyes to look at her hands in her lap. She murmurs something incomprehensible to herself.

"I beg your pardon? Can you please look at me or at least speak louder?" Linda's tone is no longer calm and focused, but upset and nervous. As she becomes aware of this, she looks again at the camera and repeats her request to Leslie in a tone that is a shade more relaxed. But Leslie refuses to make eye contact and says something louder, "I never saw them together."

The FBI agents, Frank and his son Kenneth all look at each other in surprise. Curious, they look at the screen in front of them and wait for the upcoming scenes in the other room.

"She's back in control, she's doing great! Considering what emotional rollercoaster this woman is going through!" Mayer holds his hand on his cheek and looks at Linda on the screen. Frank's deep voice fills the entire dark room in a very thoughtful tone. "She has been living in it for quite a while now. And unfortunately, not only emotionally... " Ken holds his father by the shoulder and says, encouragingly, "But she has the best savior of all times!" Frank looks into the familiar eyes. "I'm not sure about that, my boy, whether I represent her salvation or her final demise... "

Chapter 16

"You can do it! One eye at a time... Come on, it can't be that hard... After all, you´re talking already..." Rosalía, with her eyes closed, reaches her hand for the alarm clock, which seems to be ringing far away today. Grunting, she opens her eyes and realizes that she has dozed off on her couch and massacred her Highlands saga in her sleep. She picks up the book and gently pats it. "I'm sorry, I should have warned you what a restless sleeper I am... It would be interesting to know if I also chat in my sleep? Did I say something?" She smiles at her nighttime novel and lays it carefully on the stack of books next to the empty glass of wine. "It's your fault that I didn't even make it to bed! You're a bad glass! So now, all my listeners, let's see if there´s hot water today." With these words, she gets up and shuffles towards the bathroom, closing the door behind her, as usual.

"Caramba, feliz navidad! Take a quick shower before your luck runs out!"

***

Rosa stands happily at the bus stop, hardly able to believe what a great start to the day she has had so far. She started out happy and cheerful, took a hot shower, drank some coffee, ate a bit of quinoa. She even had time to put on a bit of make-up today and now she has made it to the bus stop on time! These kinds of days are just wonderful! Nothing can go wrong now because she is on the winning team. She reaches into her purse to fish for her cellphone and feels something hard. With her eyes narrowed, she slowly pulls a tube out of her purse and looks questioningly at the unfamiliar object.

"A cigar? Since when do I smoke? What are you doing in my purse?" She looks around, relieved that she´s unobserved. She twists the lid of the long tin tube and is surprised again. Slowly, she sticks her finger in the opening and pulls out the cigar, which is accompanied by a rolled paper. She looks around again as if someone is waiting for her reaction to this surprise. But there's no one paying any attention to her. She watches as the bus approaches, a bit shakily, and stops in front of her.

The door opens and an unfamiliar face nods at her in greeting. "Where´s Pedro?", she asks impulsively while putting the items back into her purse. "Buenos días, Señorita! No sé, no idea, I just got a call to jump in. Do you still want to ride if I am the driver?" He looks at her seriously, appearing to threaten to close the door in her face. "Yes, yes, of course I'll come with you!" Rosalía hops up the steps into the bus and sits down as always in the first row near the driver.

After watching the driver for a moment and worrying about what happened to Pedro, she reaches back into her purse and pulls out the rolled paper roll. Slowly she unfurls it and begins to read. A smile flits across her face as she gets lost in thought while gazing out of the moving bus.

Chapter 17

Frank watches Linda pacing back and forth in the music room with her arms crossed and looking at the ocean. Again and again, she stops briefly, shakes her head vigorously and then returns to her pacing. Frank Conley realizes he´s been looking at her ever since he took her home. In the hospital, in the intensive care unit, he had many quiet moments like this. He had studied her closely, trying to get to know her features and find out what kind of person she is. Since they've been here in his house in the Hamptons, he has had little time or energy to focus on her. An unfamiliar woman is walking the corridors of his house. He has been able to get to know Linda, spending many profound moments with her, helping her and taking care of her. Jasmine Steiner seems to be a very focused and independent woman. Although her outward appearance looks very fragile and protection-seeking, Frank has already been able to discover that a strong-willed and down-to-earth personality slumbers underneath her exterior. He wonders if she wore this style of clothing before. He sent Bonnie to get clothes for Linda after asking her about her wishes and ideas.

Now she is standing in front of him, wearing tight beige capri pants, an oversized dark brown batwing sweater and brown ballerina shoes. She has tied her dark brown hair tightly in a bun and also, for the first time, he notices that she is wearing eyeshadow and some mascara. "She looks pretty!" he thinks as he also says it out loud.

"Excuse me?" Linda takes her mind off her thoughts and faces him. Frank smiles at her, one hand in his jeans pocket, pointing with the other at his eyes. "Your make-up, it looks good on you!" He also moves his other hand in the jeans pocket, raising his eyebrows in embarrassment, while pressing his lips together.

"Oh.... Thanks, ahh... Frank!... What should we do? What should I do? None of this makes any sense. And just standing here waiting makes me CRAZY!!! I could rip out trees and throw them far away and...!" She can't finish her desperate sentence. Frank stands right in front of her, grasping her clenched fists and beaming at her. "Then let's DO EXACLTY THAT!" Confused, Linda looks at him and no more than a "Huh?" escapes her lips at that moment. He turns his demeanor from the timid schoolboy and back again to the adrenaline-flooded action hero. He stands with his legs apart in front of the big window, opens his arms as widely as he can and shouts, "Let's throw some trees! That will do us a world of good, my dear, and you will love it!"

Just as Linda opens her mouth to speak, she hears a giggle behind her. "What are YOU practicing for? Can I join in? What's the name of this game?" Susie enters the room, goes over to Linda, presses her to her bulky body and pinches her in the side.

"My sweetie, how are you? Is Bonnie´s cooking so bad? Is that why you´re so thin? Soon you will fit in my pants together with me! Oh well, that would work now, Mama´s wearing elastic!" While she babbles happily as always, she walks towards Conley, who is standing with his legs apart. She stops in front of him, copies his stance, looks up at him and winks. "Want to talk about this? Or are you undercover?" Mischievously, the well-trained actor grins at his new friend from Coney Island and kisses her affectionately on the forehead. "Nice to see you, Susie! Welcome to our think tank. We are in the process of planning the next steps."

"And tearing out trees and throwing them around are part of that?" She points to Frank, but looks at Linda, who shakes her head and raises her shoulders, saying, "I don't understand as much as you do. But I just thought it might be an English saying I´m not familiar with." Both women now look at Frank, who grins mischievously and rubs his hands like a funny cartoon character.

Chapter 18

As soon as Rosalía enters the clinic, the receptionist immediately waves to her. Puzzled, Rosa returns the nice greeting with a tentative smile. She´s heading towards the staff changing room when the receptionist makes a hissing sound and waves wildly for her to come over.

"Ah, you were beckoning me!" The good-humored physiotherapist changes her course and rushes to the reception desk.

"Buenos días, Señora! What can I do for you?"

With a raised eyebrow, the reception dragon looks at Rosa from head to toe, shaking her head, and slides the envelope towards her. She then sits down again and starts leafing through a magazine, bored.

"Muchas gracias. And you have a great day, too!" Rosa reaches for the envelope and leaves the ice-cold reception area as she walks on, wondering how many people seeking help might simply turn around and leave without having ever seen a doctor. Is this a tactic the clinic uses?... Of course, it could also be that this Gómez Hernandez is a kind, charming and extremely caring person who is simply ALWAYS having a bad moment when Rosalía passes her. She laughs out loud as this thought enters her head and then disappears in a flash into the changing room.

***

A soft sob can be heard in the sterile staircase. Slowly a door closes and through the air there comes a cautiously questioning "Hello?" The sobbing finishes with a loud nose-blowing. "Yeah, hello... Everything is good here, I'm fine!"

"Rosa? Is that you? Which floor are you on?

"No, don't! It's fine! I need a moment for myself now! But thank you!"

"But I can hear you crying! How can you be fine? What happened? I'm coming down now... "

"Mierda! Noo!!!! Please!! We'll meet in a minute, please go and get the patient file. Muchas gracias! "

Rosa waits anxiously for the sound of a door being opened but can't hear anything that sounds like that. Angry, she gets up, stomps on the floor with one leg and opens the door in front of her. "Well then, I'll go!" As she steps out, she calls back over her shoulders to the stairwell, "I'm going to IMMEDIATELY apply for another intern!"

Said and done. Or better, screamed and done! Energetic, purposeful and serious, the angry petite woman stomps out of the director's office. She looks into the secretary's amazed eyes and loses her composure, her palms flat on the desk, not holding back her tears. "He won't do it, am I right? Why me? Why do I have to do this? I can't do this! I just want to do my job well, make enough money and help Mima!" Confused, the secretary offers the now sobbing Rosalía a tissue, which she uses immediately. While offering the second tissue in a timely manner, she lays a hand on Rosalía's shoulder, who is slowly calming down, and whispers curiously, "I do not know, my dear ... what DO you have to do for the Señor Director?"

Chapter 19

"I know what he's up to!" Kenneth stands with his arms crossed over his chest in the open sliding door like a genie. Frank happily approaches his son and embraces him warmly.

"My son, it's wonderful having you here now! What do you think of my idea?" The still excited actor now holds his son by the shoulders and waits for his positive reaction. The young man grins mischievously at his father and looks at the questioning female faces in the room with a raised eyebrow.

"I'm sure you would like that, ladies. Very much, even! But..." Ken looks back at his father, who seems to miss this "but"...

"Did you just hear that? You'll be VERY pleased!"

"Toss trees? Ken? Seriously now! This is a joke, right?" Linda shakes her head and looks first at the professor, then at Susie, with her shoulders raised. Susie throws both hands over her head and walks purposefully out of the room, past the two tall men, shouting, "Bonnie?!! BOOOOOONIE!!" Frank laughs out loud heartily. "Believe me, Bonnie will be elated if you tell her about this! She will immediately drop everything and pack our bags!" He turns his gaze to Linda, beams and winks at her.

"Pack suitcases? Frank, what are you up to?"
She sits down on the chaise longue and looks
out to the sea. "You're not going away from here,
right? I can't leave now..." Sadly she rubs her
hands then starts massaging the ball of her left
thumb. A gesture she learned from Leslie back
in the Coney Island Hospital to calm her...
Leslie... The nice and caring nurse who has now
become her enemy... She immediately stops
rubbing her hand as if this tip from Leslie would
do more harm than good. She does not notice
that meanwhile Frank has come over to her and
now squats in front of her, covering her two
hands with his.

"You don't have to do anything that
repulses you. I just think a change of scenery
could do you a lot of good. And right now, there's
nothing to do here except wait. We have done
everything in our power. The videos are
broadcast nationwide, Leslie's activities are

under review, the search for Simon, Roberto and Mirjam is in full swing... You're just going crazy here... "

Linda closes her tear-filled eyes and nods slightly, "I know, but I can't go away..." She opens her eyes, letting the tears run down her cheeks, and looks at her best friend, saying, "It would be as if I let Mirjam down, and for the first time I feel like I'm close to her... Do you understand?"

"And she's right, Dad! She cannot go now. She is closer to Mirjam than ever!" Ken has sat down with the two, next to Linda on the long chaise. "If only I could finish my sentences!" He grins at his father and hugs Linda with one arm, who examines him.

"We received a call."

Chapter 20

"I still can't see everything, but if something is wrong, I notice at first glance."

Slowly, the patient rolls over onto the table that is ready for him but turns his half-open eyes towards his physical therapist. With her back to him, she mumbles something in Spanish and picks up a handkerchief. A loud, childlike snort fills the air and she apologizes. "Lo siento! I'm so sorry, that's not professional at all... I'll be right..."

"You don't have to apologize, Señorita. Crying cleanses the soul and we all need to cry once in a while. I believe you know I am a very good listener. And since I can no longer see with my eyes, what my heart and mind wish for I hear all the better. And I can keep silent like a grave..."

"No, muchas gracias, Bob, but that's not possible. I'm paid to help you. Not for you to comfort me. But that's incredibly kind of you. Really, thank you, but I'm fine now."

"I did not say that you shouldn't treat me with a wonderful massage, all the while telling me how much grief you're going through." A mischievous grin flashes on the still-swollen face of Rosalía's patient as he gently steps, one leg at a time, from the wheelchair to the floor.

"Massage? You wish, Señor! Today, hard training is on the agenda because we'll soon have company. Don't get too comfortable just yet! Today we are going to walk! Let's see if there are any muscles under those bruises. They look like a rainbow."

"Baby steps? Rainbow? Company? Which language are you speaking today, woman? Dónde está mi Rosalía? What did you do to her?" Bob puts his heavy legs back on the footstools of the wheelchair and tries to see something in the room. Right then, the door opens and a small, young, black haired man enters the room, closes the door and greets everyone. "Buenos días, I heard someone is taking their first steps here and two strong arms are needed?"

"Exactly, two STRONG arms!" Rosa looks at the little physiotherapist, surprised. "What are YOU doing here, Stefano? Where is my intern?… The tall one, with long arms and big biceps?" She points with her open hand and outstretched arm to make a point. Questioningly, she leans her head to the side.

"Well, YOU ran to the director and got rid of Simon. Now you have to make do with ME until the matter is cleared up between the two of you." He walks purposefully to the patient, who sits frozen in his chair, gently puts his hand on his shoulders and says in a reassuring voice, "She exaggerates as always! Don't you worry, it's not in the biceps. It's the right technique. You're in good hands."

"Bob?... Everything ok? Don't you feel well, Bob?!" Rosa hurries to her chalk-white patient, kneeling and feeling the pulse on his trembling wrist.

Chapter 21

"Mexico?! Those criminals! Of course, Mexico!" Susie flings her fleshy arms excitedly into the air and spins on her heels." No one is ever found in Mexico! That's like looking for a needle in a haystack!" As soon as she finishes venting her initial rage, she notices the sad faces around her, pulls her face into a look of determination and squeezes herself between Ken and Linda on the chaise longue. "But, no one can mess with us and get away with it, my beauty! It's out of the question! As Ken said, you are closer to your little mouse, even with circumstances presenting hurdles once again. But I'll eat a Mexican alive if the four of us don't manage to find those horned oxen!" She gently puts her arm around Linda's shoulder, trying to hold her tight as her friend gets up, putting both hands in her capri pockets, and goes over to the floor level window.

"Please don't talk about Roberto like that. There must be something wrong with him. He would never do that! I know him! There must be more to it; something must have happened to him." She looks out over the sea and imagines her husband's handsome, good-natured face, the way she has since recapturing her memory. Could she really draw him to her telepathically? "Ken, please report again exactly what the FBI said!" Linda crouches down, elbows on her knees, lets her head relax and wedges her hands as if in prayer, another exercise that has been shown to her by the deceptive and unscrupulous nurse.

Frank's son, the lawyer and university professor, Ken, repeats to the eager listeners the phone call, word for word, that he had with Agent Mayer with the FBI.

"Hmm..." Frank paces back and forth in the room, holding both hands at the back of his head. "It makes no sense... Unless of course... No, that would be absurd just to think it... But, after what he did to Linda???..."

"Sir?! Excuse me?" Susie is now behind Frank, tapping a finger on his muscular shoulder. "Are you studying a new role or would you be so kind as to involve us in your mental disorder?" She puts a hand on each of her hips and looks up at her friend.

"Oh... Oh... Sorry!" He puts his big hands on Susie's shoulders, squeezing them affectionately. "But of course! Well, let's assume that Simon has unscrupulously planned this whole story and Roberto did not know about it at all, but was blackmailed... Only, with what? And then again, assuming he wanted to get out... And Simon... Well... Went crazy again?"

Chapter 22

"I don't know! How many times do I have to tell you this?" Rosalía throws both hands in the air in frustration, turns on her heel and snorts to herself, "Santa Maria!!! It's like he saw a ghost! His skin turned white as chalk, his pulse went sky high and then he collapsed and lost consciousness... I... I... I have never seen anything like that... I have not even read about it...! How IS he? Is he awake? Has he said anything? I'm going to go nuts! What a shitty day today turned out to be!" The small Mexican woman falls down into the chair, puts her head in both hands, and breathes purposefully in and out.

"No, he's still sleeping, Rosa, which worries me a lot. He has already been sleeping too long. That's why I really need to know every detail, do you understand? I'm not doing this to torment you or because I don't trust your word... But the police will be here very soon an ..." The worried psychiatrist, also dressed in white, looks out the window and down onto the parking lot of the Psychiatric Center below.

"The police??? I beg your pardon? Why are the police coming here? Because of an unconscious patient? You're kidding me, Jeff?!" As if suddenly injected with energy again, Rosa jumps up from the chair, stands right next to the American Psycho, as they refer to him secretly, and stares at him with a look of determination on her face. "What's going on here? I think you all... Really ALL of you, want to drive me insane!

That's crazy! First the director because of Simon and now you because of Bob! And don't forget the enchanting genie at the reception desk who slipped me the bad news. This is indeed a madhouse! The best nut house in the world, of all time! Dios mío, you even push your employees to be committed!"

After Jeff finally gets the agitated physiotherapist to sit down again and drink a glass of water, he also sits down on a chair in front of her. He crosses his legs and folds his hands in his lap after he has neatly adjusted his tie. He makes a brief snap with his tongue, as if he had just sucked leftover food from between his teeth. Irritated by his serenity and annoyed at his disgusting gesture, Rosalía looks at him seriously, saying, "I'm sitting, I'm calm, I drank some water! Am I getting some answers here now or do I have to do a handstand first?"

Chapter 23

"I'm sorry, Bonnie. Our beloved Highlands still have to wait a bit. Instead, we will travel to Mexico. Are you coming with us? I'll get in touch with Mike right away."

While Frank throws his bag on his bed, the disappointed Scottish housekeeper steps into the walk-in closet and deliberately answers in her strong accent, "No, it's fine. I'm ok. I'll help you pack; otherwise Linda will have to wait a lot longer. The poor child, what tortures she still has to go through. How are you, Frank? We didn't have a chance to talk about it yet." She puts three neatly folded polo shirts on the big bed and turns to go back towards the closet when she is held back by Conley's hand. He looks at her lovingly. "Once I'm home again, we will treat ourselves to a single malt, eat haggis, scones and shortbread and share our thoughts, agreed? And again, I'm so sorry, Bonnie, our time was much too short. I am very interested in how YOU are doing. It is painful for both of us to always be reminded because of Linda, but there's a reason, you know... ", and they finish the sentence together.

"The universe does not make any mistakes..."

***

Mike stands by the aircraft on the small airfield behind the house and waves joyfully to his passengers. "Wonderful weather today, beautiful views and like always, thick air over Mexico City! I just got the go-ahead to fly. I hope there's no contraband coming on board! I didn't put any claims in for Customs!" Laughing, he reaches for Linda's and Frank's bags and stows them both in his flying office. Ken also hands over his bag and sits down next to the pilot's seat. "Are you piloting today, Ken?" Mike's voice is clearly heard over the headphones and Ken happily grips the helicopter controls.

"Alright! I should still find JFK, even though it's been a while since I've flown there myself! Crew, ready for takeoff?" He casts a mischievous look to the back, where Linda and his father sit, both of them giving him a thumbs up in response.

"That was not bad, my boy! For once I did not have to hold on, and I even booked a hotel. I think I should keep my eyes open for a new manager soon. Tom was not thrilled that I am... Rather WE are going to Mexico. What a feast for the paparazzi... He's just glad Susie is staying here..." Laughing, Frank holds out his hand to help Linda step out of the chopper. She starts to take her bag when Ken stops her and smiles at her, "You still have not gotten used to this?"

"In fact, I haven't... And tell me, is there ANYTHING you Conleys can't do?"

Chapter 24

"Taking a shower helps. It always helps! Get out of those clothes and under the cold shower!" Rosalía walks quickly along the sterile hall towards the staff changing rooms, her two petite hands tucked deep into her pockets, her eyes focused on the floor. She murmurs to herself, "That's crazy... Who does that? Someone made that up... Nooo... That's beyond imagination... Caramba, mundo loco! Gente horrible! Take a shower, Rosa. Taking a shower will help... "

"Mundo loco? Gente horrible? Qué pasa?" A big strong hand reaches for Rosa's arm and brings her to a halt. Irritated and once again torn from the thoughts she has been saying out loud, she looks into the eyes of her former intern. "Simon, lo siento! It's just too much for my nerves... I... I wanted to tell you myself, but you caught me today at a bad time and... And..." As if this abrupt interruption of her thoughts brings relief, the first tears slowly creep down her cheeks.

"Don't cry... Hey... What's up, Rosalía?" The big strong man, visibly shaken, pulls the little Mexican woman close to him and looks into her face with concern, wiping away her first tears. She wipes her nose on her arm and looks down at the ground. "I don't want to see you now... I CAN'T look you in the eyes right now... You just mess me up... Simon... Please understand...!" Before she can say anything else or start crying again, she feels his strong arms around her, his warm muscular chest on her wet cheek through his shirt, and his loudly beating heart in her ear.

"I understand. And you don't need to look at me, my brave girl! Gómez told me... I'm very sorry. If you want, I'll gladly bring you to him. He's still here. Unfortunately, his family can't

106

host a viewing at home." He gently caresses her back and puts his chin on her head, giving her even more support and security. A loud sob fills the hall and Rosa gives the weight of her sadness free reign. "Of course the witch tells you and everyone else in this goddamned madhouse about me!" She starts sobbing even harder. Simon guides her, holding her tightly, towards the door behind them. He opens it and walks into the small storage room with the crying Rosa still snuggled to his chest. He then closes the door behind them.

Chapter 25

Entering Mexico is a quick affair via a private gate. Linda once again sees how Frank is also a welcome guest here. The customs officers greet him heartily and his charming and loving way catches everyone's attention, as usual. Everyone is in a good mood as they get into the waiting car and, to their surprise, Tom sits next to the Mexican driver.

"What are YOU doing here?! How did you do that? Tell me, are you David Copperfield?" Frank pats his manager on the shoulder, then hugs him cheerfully. "You little hypocrite, you! First you read me the Riot Act, and then you end up bringing your own ass to the south! I can't believe this!" But before Frank can continue, Tom raises his hand in Linda's direction. "First, let me greet the lady on board. Welcome to Mexico, Linda! And once your happy companion has calmed down a bit, you're welcome to teach him some decency. I've given up on that." Then addressing Ken, he says, "Does he ever ask you where you are, or does he also call you at ungodly hours of the day and night, pour out his heart and involve you in his crazy plans, never even considering whether he's bothering you?" He looks mischievously at Frank out of the corner of his eye, clicks his tongue and murmurs, "Well, I'll get paid for it, anyway."

"Hey, amigo," Frank hisses toward the front seat, "you can't leave it that way, that's not fair!" He puts his big hand on Tom's shoulder again and asks, "Sorry, pal, you've been here already? Are you even allowed to do that? Leave the country, I mean, without informing me? What are you doing here anyway?" Curious, the action hero waits for the manager's response.

"Oh my goodness! What did you drink on that plane? Do you even take a breath between your sentences?" Laughing, Frank Conley's longtime friend and manager pats his thigh and gives instructions to the driver in fluent Spanish.

"Did he already let you know where or HOW you will spend the night, Linda?" Tom peers over his shoulder, looking for Linda's reaction. Linda re-directs her interrupted thoughts uncomfortably towards a gazing

109

audience. She suspects rightly that an answer is expected from her.

"Excuse me?" She looks from one pair of eyes to the others and Ken asks, "Everything ok, Linda?" She nods and waits for someone to repeat the original question. "What was that? Who wanted to know something about me? And why are you all staring at me?" Frank pats her playfully on the knee and answers, "Tom wanted to know if I've already made you privy to our nocturnal adventure."

Her eyes now get even bigger than they already were, and she leans back into the leather seat of the car with a slightly defensive attitude, replying, "Nocturnal adventure?! I don't know if I understand that correctly... Ken? How familiar are you with Mexican law? Should I be worried?"

Chapter 26

"Rosa?... Rosalííaaa!... Dónde estas?" The loud female voice fills the entire staff dressing room. The sound of light steps heading toward the shower cubicles can be heard, as well as repeated calls. "Rosa!! Where the heck ARE you?! The director is looking for you! The police are here! What did you do this time?! Mia madre, I can't believe you're still allowed to work here!" Carmelita throws open one shower curtain after the other and freezes at the last one as if stunned by lightning. "For heaven's sake, ROSA! What are you doing here?! What happened?!" She tries to open the shower curtain completely, but it's held in place by the motionless body just behind it. "Rosalía, MOVE RIGHT NOW! CAN YOU HEAR ME?!!" Her loud, hysterically screaming voice echoes throughout the cold room, but the person behind the curtain does not move. The warm water keeps spraying down on them, wafting humid steam.

111

"Mierda, mierda, mierda! Then I'll just get the maintenance guy! He can get you out of here and give you a spanking!" As she tries to stomp out angrily, she stops for a fraction of a second, turns her head over her shoulder towards the shower stall and smiles, walking slowly to the door, opening it and shouts, "Or better yet, I'll get Simon! The big, strong, good-looking SIIIMMOON!!!!" She waits a moment and hears something from the shower. "Leave me alone! I'm FINE! Don't you DARE get ANYONE! I just want to take a shower in peace, that's all! Comprendes?"

Shaking her head, the grinning nurse closes the door of the changing room and walks triumphantly back to the showers. "In your work clothes?! You want to take a shower in your work clothes? Wow, you're by far the craziest chick fluttering around in this damn madhouse! What's wrong with you? And what the heck have you been up to? Spill the beans! What's going on?" When she reaches the last stall, she stops again in front of the half-opened curtain, puts both hands on her hips, and taps her foot against the shower stall. "I'm on shift and can't stay here and babysit you for hours! You coming?... Or should I tell the Señor Director to lock you up in a straitjacket?"

The shower is turned off and the curtain opens from the inside. Rosalía, the small, usually joyful physiotherapist stands there in her soaked white scrubs, wet hair sticking to her face and shoulders. Carmelita peaks between her hands, which are now covering her face, "Mierda! Look at you!! Are you crazy?!!"

Chapter 27

Linda is standing in her hotel room with her mouth open wide, not believing her eyes. She slowly turns in a circle, still not able to breathe. Slowly she approaches the oversized netted curtain and looks at the sea in front of her. Between her and this natural beauty is a terrace with a small mosaic whirlpool, a hammock attached to two wooden posts and a cozy sitting area with a covered basket lounger. Behind her, in the open space, there is a hanging wooden bed, an open bathroom overlooking the sea and behind it, the jungle. Never in her entire life has Linda been in a hotel room floating in the air on stilts. Her first tree house visit.

"Well? How do you like it, my dear?" Frank steps silently into the dream tree house. Conforming to the Conley mannerisms, he stands next to her, with his legs apart, his hands crossed under his armpits, and lets his gaze glide over the blue expanse. "We came here every year. She loved this place. She could linger on the patio, in the pool, or sitting in the basket chair with her nose stuck in a book for hours. I think that was pretty much the only place it did not matter if I was gone on a shoot, spending days on the road. She said a week here was worth more to her than a summer in the Bahamas." A loving smile flits across Frank's face as he talks about these memories.

"What was she like, Frank?" Linda whispers these words timidly, as if she does not want to end this moment in which her life saver speaks about his deceased wife to her for the first time.

The tall man looks sideways at the petite woman next to him, as a huge smile radiates across his entire face. "Kenneth is the male image of her! That's exactly how she looked; but slightly smaller and of course not so muscular." He laughs with amusement at these words. "But otherwise, he's just like Heather!"

Linda quietly repeats the name and looks timidly at the widower. "Can you tell me how she died?" Frank's body tightens and cramps up as

115

he puts both his hands in his pockets, looks toward the sea, and with no emotion, answers, "I killed her."

Chapter 28

"You want to hug me?! Ok, one thing is clear now: You belong in this nuthouse! But not as an employee – as a patient! Mierda! And I just now almost shit my pants from sheer worry and panic! Go freshen yourself up – you look like a smashed cucaracha! And el Señor Director is not waiting for you with a margarita on a golden tray! You crazy nut job!" Carmelita is clearly infuriated and waves her hands in the air as she stomps over to her locker. "And it's all YOUR fault that my makeup is now a complete mess! How in the world did you ever find a job? Or complete your education? Is everyone in your family this crazy or are you a 'special edition'? Mierda! Unbelievable!" She tears open her small beauty bag and rummages around in it. With an eyeliner pencil in her hand, she points menacingly towards the shower stalls, where water is once more running. "Do you have any idea whatsoever how many people would envy you? I mean, I MYSELF would have nothing against it... What in the WORLD does he see in you? He must have a thing for crazy women! Where does he come from anyway? Hey, cucaracha, don't spread this far and wide!!" While Carmelita screeches loudly at her image in her cosmetic mirror, Rosalía exits the shower. With a towel wrapped around herself, she slowly walks toward her locker, her head hanging down.

"I am certain you will make sure everyone knows..." she murmurs softly to herself and takes some fresh clothes out of the locker. She quickly puts on her panties and bra and wraps herself in a work smock.

"Qué dices?" her work colleague asks as she comes over and sits next to her on the bench. "Nothing, forget it! Just try to keep it to yourself, ok? It's embarrassing enough for me already!" The physiotherapist rubs cream into her face, then takes a comb and starts combing her wet hair. The curious nurse sitting next to her bends backwards, leaning on her hands to get a better look at her bust, and pops a bubble gum bubble. "Tell me more! Is he a good kisser? Is he wild? Gentle? Does he bite? Are his eyes open or closed?" A mischievous smile flits over her lips and she chews even more eagerly on her strawberry bubble gum.

"Stop that! That's gross!" Rosalía throws the wet towel at her. "You know perfectly well that that's not allowed on the unit! Besides, you look like a cow chewing its cud!"

"Ha!" replies Carmelita, catching the towel nimbly, and continues, "but making out in the supply room during work hours IS allowed here, then?" She stands up, throws the towel back at her colleague, and heads for the door. "I don't have any more time anyway for your crazy stories and your mentally ill brain! I have patients out there who actually need my help. And you'd better hurry, like I said. El Señor Director is looking for you! Yet AGAIN! Is your salary actually higher than mine? I will have to look into that – that would be the cherry on top with all the crap you are obviously doing here!" She opens the door to enter the corridor, but her path is suddenly blocked by an angry balding man.

Chapter 29

Linda stares at Frank with an unblinking look. "Why are you saying that? That's not at all true!" She walks with short, slow steps towards the man, who is still standing there, motionless, and has no idea if she should touch him. His stiff

119

stance and his staring gaze make her hesitate for a second, but then she puts her hand gently on his arm. This touch seems to tear him out of some deep abyss, where his thoughts were wandering miles away. He flinches and looks directly into Linda's brown eyes, saying, "Because that's the truth, Linda. Because I alone am responsible for her death. And that's not even the whole story." He goes into the room and stops in front of the suspended bed. He takes the cord that is holding up the bed in his hand, looks at it and makes the bed swing a little. Then he turns back towards Linda and presses his lips together. An expression comes onto his face that Linda has never seen before, but that tells her how painful his thoughts must be right now.

The loud knock on the door, which sounds like a hammer banging on a glass pane, makes the two of them jump. After five similar knocks, the door slowly opens and two happy

120

eyes blink into the sunny room. "Who wants a margarita before we start up the beast?" Linda and Frank both turn quickly and reply as one, saying, "Susie?!" Her voluptuous happiness now spreads over her entire frame and she spreads her arms wide. "You didn't seriously believe I would leave you in the lurch here, did you? One for all, all for one!" On her way over to embrace Linda, she pinches the big actor on his waist and winks at him. "Robin Hood is a role you would be great at! You would look gorgeous in pantyhose!" She gives Linda a quick hug and Susie now appears irritated. She looks at the two people standing before her. "Ooookaaay... What's going on here? My sensory skills are as good as a rattlesnake's and I smell tension. He didn't escape us, did her??!!" She grabs hold of Linda's arm as if she's about to fall over. "That cannot be! We all got here as quickly as possible and Leslie is still behind bars, so she couldn't have warned him..." She cannot finish her angry sentence because Frank is waving his hand at her.

"All right, all right! Nobody escaped us! We are just leaving. But you know what, Susie? A margarita is a fantastic idea! And because YOU are here, it's an even BETTER idea! Let me hug you or I will be offended because I am already your second choice anyway!" The two friends hug each other tightly and the strong action hero lifts feisty Susie up a bit. She screeches loudly and slaps him on the shoulder. "Put me down, you creep! I'm not a hussy!" Once she's standing on her own two feet again, she smoothes her flower-patterned dress and straightens her glasses hanging from a chain on her neck. "As if I were such easy prey! Phooey! And stupid on top of it! I want you to tell me right now what was going on here before Mr. Universe tried to seduce me!"

Chapter 30

"Is she in there?!" Carmelita jumps as the angry director snaps at her, then peeks past her into the women's locker room. Carmelita bravely continues to chew her gum, maintaining her position in front of the small bald man, and replies, "Sí, Señor Director. She's just getting freshened up and will go to your office IMMEDIATELY afterwards, just as you asked." She says this so loudly that Rosa is certain to hear her. "Freshening up? Why would she need to freshen up? She needs to immediately…"

"Here I am, Señor Director. I was just on my way to your office." The physiotherapist, freshly showered, hair brushed, and clean clothes on, now stands directly behind the nurse, who cannot hide a mischievous grin. "Yes, just freshened up, Señorita… Or rather Señora, of course!" She blows a bubble with her gum and salutes the two of them as her goodbye. "I have to go back to the station. My work here is done. Adiós and good luck!" She winks at Rosa and strolls calmly down the corridor.

"Lo siento mucho, mucho Señor Director! That is absolutely not my style and I am deeply ashamed of this, from the bottom of my heart!" Please let me explain..." The small Mexican woman, who is speaking from her heart and extremely embarrassed, is interrupted by a chopping movement of her boss' hand, whose face is still red. "I don't give a damn what you need to explain to me! When I ask that you come to my office, you need to come immediately, even if you have a half-dead patient on your table! I am the boss here and I say who does what when and where! Do you understand?!" He holds his rage-filled face so close to hers that she can smell the stench of his unbearable halitosis. This makes her stomach feel even queasier than it already did. She holds on to the doorframe with one hand, which infuriates the small fat baldy even more. "Oh, so I'm boring you now?! So let's go find out what the police think about waiting for la Señorita so long! They've been in my office for quite a while now! And I guarantee you: If my institution should get a bad image because of YOUR unreliability, I will make sure that you never get a job anywhere in Mexico for the rest of your life!" He turns on his heels and stomps down the corridor. The intimidated physiotherapist follows him, her head down and shoulders slumped.

***

In the Director's spacious office, two uniformed men sit on the leather sofa. A man wearing a black suit stands at the window, looking out. For a fraction of a second, Rosa thinks that this room would be much more suitable as a treatment room than the one she is currently allowed to use. This thought dissolves with a gesture by the man in the suit. He moves

125

to stand in front of her and extends his hand. "Buenos días, Señora! I am pleased to finally meet you in person. El Señor Director has told me only good things about you! I would like to start by telling you how much we appreciate you working with us in a most professionally confidential way." He holds her hand in both of his this entire time, and squeezes it a bit tighter before finally releasing it.

Confused and full of questions, Rosalía looks at him and is barely able to get her first question out. "We're working together? I, I don't quite understand…" This isn't the first time she's been confused today, and she looks towards the Director for help, who is now sitting comfortably on the leather chair behind his huge desk. As if caught red-handed, he immediately puts a beaming smile on his face and laughs happily. "Rosalía, my dear soul! You already know it, but these are the men from the FBI!"

Chapter 31

"Well, sit down and I'll tell you what happened." Frank Conley sits on the suspended bed, resting his forearms on his thighs and folding his hands as if in prayer. Susie still does not understand what this is all about, but obeys and sits down next to Linda in a bamboo chair. Both women stare intently at the person speaking, who is struggling to find the right words. Linda notices his agitated mood and decides not to torment him any longer with her curiosity. "Let it go, Frank! You don't have to tell us now! We'll find the right time for this, if that's what you prefer." She gets up from her chair and tries to get by Frank on her way to the door, but he grabs her by the hand before she can go past him. "It's been the right time for weeks now, Linda! Please, sit down and listen to me. I think you should know everything about me."

Linda sits down, a questioning look appearing on her face, and looks expectantly into the sad eyes of this man who saved her life. "Nothing will change between us, Frank, if I listen to this story, right? Because if so, I beg you not to tell it to me NOW! I cannot stand any more!" Tears fill her eyes, but she does not look away from Conley.

After a few tense moments, the usually hyperactive Susie slaps her thighs, leans forward in her chair, and looks from one person sitting next to her to the other. "Hellloooo?!... What the heck is going on here? Have you both gone crazy?! What in the world is going on? Caramba! I don't recognize either one of you! What did I miss?!" She rises awkwardly from the bamboo chair. "Modern hotel chairs!" She walks over to Frank. "What have you done that's so bad that it makes her cry now? What do you have to confess to her?" She then turns to Linda and says, "What could change between you two? What are you afraid of? PLEASE! Tell me what is going on and stop refusing to tell each other, and especially ME, what is going on! Susie cannot stand that!" She gestures uncontrollably with her hands in the air, as if slapping at mosquitoes.

Frank lowers his head and answers quietly, "Linda asked me about my wife and I was just about to tell her how she died." The pink fades slowly from Susie's face and her face takes on a sad expression. She sits down next to Frank, puts her arm around his shoulders, and purses her lips. She then says, "Hmmm... I understand... Excuse my insensitive ways... But tell me, my big boy, why NOW? Why do you feel the need to tell this story NOW?"

"Because I'm selfish and I always have been!" Frank Conley stands up from the bed angrily, goes over to Linda, kneels down in front of her, takes her two delicate hands in his large ones, and looks at her pleadingly. "Please Linda...! I must tell you about this!"

Chapter 32

Rosalía listens attentively to the man in the suit, sits down slowly on the leather chair behind her, and covers her mouth with both hands. She then looks first at the Director, whose lips are pursed and who is nodding with his eyes closed. She then looks back at the agent. Her eyes slowly fill with tears until there's no room and then they slowly spill down her cheeks. She swallows loudly, wiping away the first tear and then the three that follow, looking down at her hands, which are now cramped together in her lap. The thin man in the suit kneels down in front of the distraught woman, puts his warm hand on hers, and looks up at her questioningly. "I can understand that this information is very shocking. But do you now understand how incredibly important it is for us to get EVERY individual detail from you?" To put a bit more power behind his question, he squeezes Rosalía's hands gently but firmly together. She nods slightly and inhales through her nose. She apologizes, pulls her hands out of his and reaches into the pocket of her medical smock. She pulls out a rolled up piece of paper, realizes that it's not the handkerchief she expected to find, and quickly puts the paper back into her pocket. She looks around her, as if caught in a trap and slowly pulls a handkerchief from that same pocket.

"But I can't tell you any more than what I have already told you." She tugs nervously at her sleeve and looks down, tilting her head slightly to one side and muttering, "He claims to have been an operations assistant. For some reason I cannot put into words, I believe him. I am convinced he has worked in heal + care or nursing because he seems to understand so much. He has practical experience that simply cannot be learned from books."

She now looks directly into the agent's eyes and adds quietly, "English is certainly not his native language. But you probably already found that out yourself." Slightly ashamed of her stupidity, she looks down at the floor again and bites her lips.

"It's not? Then what is his native language?" The agent glances at his colleagues in the room and then looks with interest at Rosalía. "You know, Señorita, the thing is…He's not talking to anyone, except with you apparently!" He opens his hands and holds them out to her, as if to present something to her. Surprised, the now astonished Mexican woman looks around her. "Excuse me? That's impossible! Nowhere in his records does it say that he doesn't speak. It does say that he cannot see, but that he doesn't speak? You must have misunderstood! Why would he hide this?"

"That's EXACTLY what we want to find out, my dear."

Chapter 33

As Kenneth enters the tree house, he looks from person to person, confused. "What's going on here? What happened? Dad?" His gaze stops on the action hero, who sits on the hanging bed, his shoulders tense, his hands folded, and tears in his eyes. He raises his head, looks at his surprised son, and replies, "I told them..." His explanation is interrupted by Susie jumping out of her chair like a fury and approaching him with quick steps.

She stops in front of him and he is not sure if she wants to sneak past or hug him. Since she does neither, he slowly stands up and looks down at his small, roundish friend. She takes another step closer to him, looks up at him, squeezes her eyes into slits and points her forefinger threateningly close to his face. "Now you listen to me, you big... big... man... you!" She hisses the words through thin lips. "Not AGAIN, do you understand? Not a SINGLE time more do I want to hear such a terrible lie! I absolutely cannot stand liars! No, even worse – I despise them! I avoid them like the plague! I banish them from my life! And you are NOT a liar, right, Frank Conley? You are not, right?" Her furious words and appearance are extremely threatening and Frank almost cannot recognize the usually funny, happy Susie now. He shakes his head slightly, barely noticeably, and raises his shoulders. "Unfortunately, Susie, I am not lying. I wish I were lying, but..." She takes her small round fist and smacks him in the stomach with it, interrupting him mid-sentence, saying, "You should not lie! It was an accident! A terrible, horrible, tragic accident!" She now throws her arms around Frank's waist and presses her head into his chest. "Oh Frank, I am so terribly, terribly sorry! What you had to go through – no one would wish that on their worst enemy! But I beg you, it was an accident! You are not at fault – you did not kill her!"

Linda is now standing next to them and puts her hand on Frank's arm. "I am also sorry, Frank. And I am deeply honored to be allowed to have the name of your unborn daughter. But you are judging yourself too harshly! You did what you could to save both of them – you didn't kill them. It was a terrible accident! You are not to blame for that drunkard driving at that moment, please Frank! What does this have to do with selfishness? I have never met such a selfless, helpful person as you! Look at me! I would be dead, rotting and devoured by animals if you and your big heart did not exist! Fine! If you call all of your good will towards me 'selfish' then so be it!

Here is what I think, your 'selfishness' helped bring me back to life and is now helping me to bring back my Mirjam! For your 'selfishness' I only have gratitude!" Linda's voice has grown louder and more firm with each word, making Ken step closer to her and put his hand on her shoulder. She looks from father to son, saying, "Ken, please, say something! How can he be allowed to keep tormenting himself like this?"

Ken looks at his father sadly. Frank presses his lips firmly together, closes his eyes and whispers into the room, "What the press does not know, and what I have kept secret until now... That night, there was not just ONE drunkard at the wheel..."

Chapter 34

Squeezed like an acidic lemon, the small physiotherapist drops onto the wooden bench behind the clinic. She lies down on it lengthwise and takes a moment to squint into the warm sunshine before she closes her eyes. Thousands of thoughts are racing wildly through her mind and she struggles to concentrate on just one of them. "What a big mess you have gotten yourself involved in, Señorita! Am I so obviously a señorita? My GOODNESS! It's like I'm an unpopped kernel of corn instead of a piece of popcorn. Goddamn it! I AM a piece of popcorn and not a señorita! I am not even a good girl! I can get angry too! Yessir! Now, concentrate, you bad piece of popcorn! This is doing us no good at all. We need clear thoughts now, one right after the other! So, let's start from the beginning!" Keeping her eyes closed and holding her hands up in the air, as if showing someone the way, she continues speaking out loud. "Bob survived a terrible, horrible... Ohhh, just an awful accident! He can no longer see or walk. However, he will not talk about it... Why not? He thinks he was a surgical assistant in

New York, but he speaks English with an accent. Jeff, the psychiatrist, says Rohypnol drops could create these kinds of side effects... But why won't he talk to anyone besides me? And who the hell did the FBI bring into the situation? And who was that today? Stefano came through the door, so I didn't pay attention to Bob for a second, and bam!" She claps her hands together, opens her eyes, jumps up from the bench as if bitten by a tarantula, as a look of horror fills the green eyes that are now so familiar to her.

You said, "Never stop!" Simon holds both of his hands innocently in front of his muscular chest and smiles tenderly at her. "How is my temptress doing?" He wants to take her into his arms, but she holds him off with an outstretched arm. "I'm going to die!" is her short, breathless response. Shocked, her intern bends down and says, "Pardon me? What do you mean you're going to die?" He tries to touch her again, but she pushes him away, sits down on the bench and takes a deep breath. "I will die because of you! You will bring me to my grave earlier than I had planned, Simon. I can't do this. I imagined everything much differently. I don't want it to be like this…" She shakes her head before resting it on her hands. She slowly squeezes her face tightly and groans. She then bounces back onto her feet and shakes her entire body. "I'm going crazy! Right now! Watch and learn how a person can go insane from one moment to the next!"

Laughing, Simon claps his hands and cheerfully shouts at the tiny Mexican woman, "Well, from one moment to the next, that is not what I would diagnose in YOUR case, popcorn!" He follows this with another attempt at getting close to her, but this is interrupted by a single punch to his stomach. "How long have you been here?! I'm going to die!!!!" Rosie lies down theatrically on the bench and covers her face with her hands. "Why me? Dios mío! Why me? I have always been a good Catholic, caring for others, studying and working diligently. I have not really cursed all that much and I have never gotten involved with any indecent men, and now this mess!! I simply do not deserve this!"

"None of us deserve anything like this, my beauty!" Simon now sits next to her, puts his hand on her ankle and adds, "But I don't deserve to be called a 'mess.' I will simply not stand for that!" He squeezes her ankle gently and looks at her. "That was nice today… I wanted to tell you that before you took off and then I couldn't find you anywhere… Do you want to explain to me what is really going on?"

Chapter 35

The mood in the car has become unbearable, so Tom decides to say something. "Who would enjoy a tasty margarita right about now? Susie, didn't you want to bring these two over here for this or did I once again miss happy hour?" Frank dutifully replies, "You haven't missed anything, Tom. I'm sorry that we're all in such a poor mood. I had to tell the ladies the truth about Heather and Linda. So I think a round of margaritas would not be very appropriate right about now. Let's go to the station and find out what they have for us. What is going on with you, Jasmine?" He turns his serious gaze to the Swiss woman's tear-stained face and everyone waits anxiously for her reaction. She has never heard her real name – Jasmine – spoken by the man who saved her ever since she shared her memory on the Coney Island jetty. She looks at him for a long time before answering. "I agree with you, Frank, as far as the drinks are concerned, but nothing changes the fact that Jasmine no longer exists. Let's go straight to the station and find my baby, please!"

She smiles at him in forgiveness, puts her cold, trembling hand on his, and whispers, "I will never forget what you've done already and what you continue to do for me. And even for your own selfish reasons. I owe you my life and hopefully my entire future with my daughter..."

"But I, I... I would love to have a drink! Honestly! Am I the only one who wants to fire up this steamy situation and disinfect my throat?!" Susie's alert nature has returned and she looks to Kenneth, the sensible son who is also a lawyer, for help. "Ken, please, help an old, helpless, innocent lady get a drink! You're a good boy – I know you are – you won't make me stay sober in this situation just because the two of them agree!" She now waves her finger back and forth threateningly around the interior of the vehicle, looking around. "Otherwise, this cat will get dangerous with the police, and you don't want that, right? It would be much better to make her purr!"

Before anyone else can react, Tom taps the driver on the shoulder and gives him brief instructions in Spanish, which he confirms with a wave of his hand in the direction he is supposed to drive. Then he turns around to look behind him and shakes his head. "Why do you keep talking about the police and a police station? We aren't going to drive to either one. But no one will pay any attention to me! First let's put one down. Miss Manders had it right – I cannot bring you there when you're all in this mood. They will throw all of you in the loony bin together!" He raises his eyebrows and faces forward again, now speaking to the windshield. "Just take a look at these surprised faces!"

Chapter 36

"But you know that Pablo is dead." The tiny woman sobs softly, keeping her eyes closed. Simon moves closer to her and caresses her leg.

"But why is this bothering you so much? What did this Pablo guy mean to you?" Rosalía pulls her legs in closer to her body and hugs them with both arms. "Pablo is... Pablo was... the best bus driver Mexico has ever seen. He was my friend, my morning companion, my faithful soul, my Wailing Wall. He was like a father to me. The father I never had..." The giant tears roll slowly out of her reddened eyes and she wipes them with the back of her hand. "It's okay, let them out. Tears cleanse your soul, and that's good! What happened exactly with Pablo? How did he die?"

Rosalía sits up, now moving closer to Simon, as if seeking protection from him. She tells him about Pablo's injury, the treatment he received too late, and the blood poisoning, which took away all his will to live. "I was not there for him... Too late... I had no more energy! I should have looked in on him every day! I am certain he was in great pain and I – the stupid, idiotic cow that I am – was completely focused on me and my own problems! Oh, what a fool I am! As if my dreams in this madhouse could ever come true! But Pablo! Yes, Pablo took every unrealistic dream of mine seriously... He took ME seriously... Can you believe THAT?" She laughs hysterically, fake-laughing, and leans her head back. "Take ME seriously... That's a waste of time for every honest and faithful soul, like Pablo... You should stay far away from me, Simon! I am dangerous... Deadly dangerous!" The tears start flowing again down her sad face, but she now carelessly lets them fall.

Before she can open her eyes, hearing nothing from her listener in reply, she feels his warm, soft lips on her neck. His lips kiss her softly all down her neck and she can feel his light breath stroking her skin. Goose bumps spring up over her entire body, her heart starts to race, and her blood feels as if it's boiling in her veins. She can feel her pulse quicken and knows that

Simon can also feel it in her neck. She doesn't dare move but takes a deep breath to avoid the threat of fainting. He lays his big hand on her neck, slides it down over her shoulder, down her arm to her hand, embracing her warmly and protectively. He kisses the tears on her cheek, her nose, and – very gently – her mouth. A touch of his lips, a tender closeness that makes her glow. She opens her mouth and starts to kiss him back, when she hears his soft voice, whispering as if far away. "What did the police want with you?"

Chapter 37

The tense mood starts to slowly disappear in the small local restaurant. After Frank gets everyone to get through their selfie attack, he sits next to his son, smiles, grabs him around the neck and hugs him. "See, my boy? Your old man is not too old for the right fans!"

Then, turning to Tom, he says, "Hey, Tom, they are waiting for a movie to come out in Mexico!" He laughs and turn to Susie, winking at her, as he says, "Well, my sweetie, how about a supporting role? Then we will let the strange night owl take on the day shift also!" He leans on the table and wraps his hand around the margarita glass in front of him.

The cheerful receptionist from Coney Island Hospital sips from her glass contentedly, then places it like a golden goblet on the table and brushes an imaginary strand of hair off of her face like a movie star. "I know, I know, Hollywood has been waiting a long time for this sexy talent... But unfortunately, I will have to disappoint you all. This star will shine in another sky. Coney Island needs me even more. Susie has the nose, you know, that certain something! She feels and sees things that no one else can! I have now turned into an indispensable employee. Or why do you all think I can just take off for Mexico without a moment's notice? I know things that our top committee would never find out about without me... And of course it never will... They just don't know it yet... But what I actually want to say, if this margarita would stop interrupting me all the time..." She takes another sip from her glass and looks at Linda. "I love my job, and over the past few months, it has become clear to me how important it is." Then she turns to Frank and Tom. "You just keep doing your thing without me. That show at the airport was enough for me! This normal person here has no fear of showing up at the door with no makeup on and in her bathrobe. I am the American dream of every man, understand? This is pure mind cinema that belongs in the real world!" She lifts her index finger in the air, winks and clicks her tongue.

Linda smiles at her new friend and says, "How right you are, Susan Manders! What would Coney Island be without you! And where would I be without you! Thank you!" She raises her glass to toast a round. Everyone else does the same and Kenneth says a toast. "To the true heroes of this story and to the real world! To the friendship at this table! To Mirjam!" They clink their glasses together. "To Mirjam!" Franks says this loudly, taking a big gulp from his glass. He then slams it back on the table and looks directly into Linda's eyes. "How are you feeling? Are you scared?" Linda also sets her glass on the table and returns his gaze. "I am scared to death, Frank! What if she is no longer alive! She was... She was born prematurely...! What if I meet Roberto? Nothing is the way it used to be... I MYSELF am no longer the same person I was before..." Frank puts his warm hand on hers and looks at her with understanding. "I understand you very well... But you know, fear is good... Fear can be very helpful... It keeps you alert and prepared. And even if Mirjam only has half of your genes, she is also a fighter. I am so certain that we will be taking your little one home with us!"

Chapter 38

Angry and disappointed, Rosalía stomps down the long, sterile corridor in the basement. "Ignorant fool! What is he thinking anyway! Phony stunning looks won't cut it here, amigo! After all, you're not Zorro! Or, or Connor MacLeod... Yeah, THEY would know how to treat and protect a lady. Where have all the good heroes gone? Are there really only these wannabe cool guys with nothing behind their masks but limitless self-love? I feel sick..." She leans against the wall with one hand and closes her eyes for a moment. The lights in the corridor start to flicker and she feels a cool breeze. She opens her eyes, blinks, and looks down the corridor. "Simon?... Hello?... Pablo? Is that you?" The lights continue to flicker and as if someone

150

has opened a door, she feels the breeze again. "Could it be? Pablo… I am going to visit you now… Or whatever is left of you on this earth…" She rummages in her pocket and takes out a piece of paper. She unfolds it, reads the number written on it out loud, and looks at the room number in front of her. "You're not far away…" She says this out loud as she walks past several doors and stops in front of a closed door with the same number as on her piece of paper. She takes a deep breath and pushes the door to enter the wake.

***

Her eyes red and puffy from crying, Rosalía comes out again after a long farewell and stands in the corridor. She puts her flat hand on the closed door and nods with confidence. She straightens her back, lifts her chest, and walks down the corridor with her head held high, her steps determined. She clenches her hands into fists, extends her arms, and hisses through her full lips. "No more messes, chaos and sadness... Caramba! It would be laughable if I couldn't do this!" She bangs her fist against the wall and immediately grabs that hand with her other, rubbing it. "No, not with force, but with confidence and respect! How many people are there in this world? Seven billion? Eight? Does anyone else on this planet feel lost?... No, Rosalía, that's not how you were raised... NO ONE should feel bad! NO ONE should feel lost... You absolutely cannot say that – not even think it! Now you need to take care of all your pending matters. You need to finish up everything that needs to be finished up. Then you can finally dare to take the next step!"

She spends a long time wiping away the last of her tears, thinking about her personal oath to herself, and then blows her tiny nose. She starts walking towards the door that leads to the fire escape, but then pauses. "Phooey!

Forget the fitness training for today! Today is my day off, isn't it, Pablo?" She turns 180 degrees and walks down to the other end of the corridor. She then presses the button for the elevator as if her finger were doing this for the first time ever. She enters the elevator when it arrives and lets it take her to the fourth floor, thinking to herself, "Inside here, no one would be able to hear you..."

Chapter 39

"Oh holy, crazy professor!!! If you are not crazy yet, you will certainly get that way very quickly if you are brought here! How is this even possible – that something like this would be allowed!" With both hands on her cheeks, eyes wide open, Susie looks with horror out of the car. Linda also has a look of surprise on her face. The three gentlemen stare dumbfounded at the shabby building in front of them. Frank is finally able to speak again. "Are you sure this is the right place, Tom? We must have come to the wrong address… This cannot be…" Tom turns to look into the back seat and nods. "I am sorry, my friends, this is it!"

The driver lets his passengers get out of the fancy vehicle and Tom gives him new instructions. "We will go through the back entrance. It's better, according to the driver, and the head of the institution is already waiting for us. As little attention as possible, of course. Money-hungry fool!" Tom shakes his head as he walks towards the building. Linda grabs him by the arm. "What do you mean? What does this have to do with money?"

"EVERYTHING here revolves around the love of money! Everyone wants to have it, but no one wants to do much to get it! We are paying the director of this lunatic asylum to give us all the information he has without informing the local police. Although somehow I just don't trust the man…" Tom squeezes his eyes into tiny slits and looks up at the building. "He said, 'No policía, prometido'… But I could hear his grin even through the phone…"

They are able to open the door at the back entrance with no one noticing them and Tom shakes his head. "Imagine such safety measures at home!" Linda, Susie and Kenneth follow closely on his heels. Frank first observes their surroundings, taking another look at the parking lot as if he were on the set of one of his films, except that no cameras are pointing at him. Before he even sets one foot into the building, he sees a mental health employee out of the corner of his eye. Or at least he assumes this based on the man's white clothing. He waits for the employee's reaction and takes a quick glance at his face. The man quickly turns around, waves his hand as if he has forgotten something and heads towards the parking lot.

155

Conley's forehead creases as he watches the white smock-clad man.

"Dad? Are you coming?" Frank hears Ken's voice from inside the building and tears himself away from his observations. He casts one final glance at the figure outside before he follows the others inside. "I'm coming!" As he walks toward his son, Ken asks him, "Are you okay, Dad?"

"Everything is fine with me. I just thought there was someone out there who somehow seemed familiar to me."

Chapter 40

"So, who do we have here? Hola, you nut! Did you get lost? Has it gotten to the point where you don't even remember where YOUR department is located? You are on the fourth floor right now. This is the hospital ward... For physical illnesses, in addition to the mental. You, my young nut case, are supposed to go up one more floor to the CLOSED ward!?" Carmelita speaks these last words louder and more clearly than her previous bluster. She looks at Rosalía with her eyebrows raised, continues munching on her chewing gum as usual, and puts both of her hands on Rosa's slim waist. "Say something, what are you doing here?" Rosalía, not allowing herself to be intimidated, forces her way past the intrusive nurse. But she cannot resist and gently pushes her shoulder. This gesture obviously surprises Carmelita and she throws her arms theatrically into the air. "Ah yes, of course! We have just barely reeled the male heart throb in and suddenly we feel brave! This is not like you! Do you hear me? This is not your league, cucaracha!"

As if this poisonous snake who is clearly seeking a fight had heard these thoughts, Rosa once again hears her voice. "You don't even know which room he is in!" She has barely finished her sentence when Rosalía suddenly stops walking and without turning around, she asks, "So will you help me find it?" She hears the slow steps of the nurse as she walks in her direction. Carmelita walks slowly around Rosalía and stops right in front of her. The sweet smell of her chewing gum wafts between them like a delicate veil and they stare at each other.

"I'll show you which room your favorite patient is in and you leave Simon to me! You tell me all about him, what I need to know, and you stay away from him!" Rosalía has to force a broad grin from appearing on her face and only nods seriously. "Well okay... Whatever you want. I will have to agree to this deal. It won't be easy... But hey, he is actually MUCH better suited to you, right? Good looking, intelligent, clever, seductive, ambitious and successful! A male image of you! It would not have gone well between him and me for long anyway... After all,

I'm just a little gray mouse…!" Obviously pleased with this realization and agreement on the part of Rosalía, Carmelita's face begins to radiate joy and she places her bony hand on Rosalía's shoulder. "Well, well, it's not so hard to see yourself as you truly are, eh cucaracha? You'll find your soulmate someday… Room 5… But don't jump all over him right now. He has just regained consciousness!"

Chapter 41

"Señor Conley! It is a great honor and pleasure for me to welcome you here with us! Please take a seat! And your friends as well, bienvenidos a México! What can I offer you to drink? Coffee? Tea? A tequila?" The excited director whirls around Frank, as well as around his own axis, barely taking a breath between sentences. Frank looks down at the small bald head, raising his eyebrows. He then looks at

Tom, shaking his head, and offers Linda and Susie each a spot on the leather sofa. "Ladies first… At least that's what I was taught as a child in Scotland. Other countries, other customs, right?" With a smile, he waits for the tiny fat man's embarrassed reaction before sitting down next to Linda.

"Oh, of course, please excuse me, ladies! Por favor, discúlpenme!" He slaps his chest with his right hand and lowers his head as if he were about to be knighted. "We are not used to having such famous celebrities in the building. This, this makes me a bit confused. Would it be completely inappropriate for me to ask for an autograph or for a photo, Señor Conley?" Embarrassed, he first looks at Linda, then at Frank.

"You know what? That's a great idea! Once we have discussed what we should do next here and what information you have for us, we can take some beautiful photos together and relax a bit!" Frank leans his forearms on his legs, rubbing his hands together, and gives the little man a serious stare. "I see you have kept your promise and haven't informed the police about our arrival... That's true, right, Señor Director?" The director nods eagerly and walks to his desk with small steps. He picks up a file and starts to take it over to Frank. But Frank waves him away immediately and points to his son, Kenneth. "Please, may I introduce you to Kenneth Conley, my son and lawyer." Visibly astonished, the director of the institution looks at Ken, reaches his moist hand out in greeting, and hands him the file with his other hand. Ken shakes the director's hand politely and takes the bundle of papers.

"Could I please have a glass of water?" asks Linda. "My mouth is very dry. Maybe it's the heat – I'm sorry." She points to her mouth as if to illustrate her thirst. "But of course, Señora!" The small Mexican man quickly reaches for the water bottle on his table and the glass next to it. He walks across the room to her, holding both items in his hands. Frank takes them from him and fills the glass before handing it to Linda. "Are you... Well, I mean... are YOU looking for someone here?" The still very nervous-looking host addresses this question to Linda. Closing her eyes and nodding, she lets the soothing liquid revive her dry mouth and throat. As soon as she has swallowed the last drop, she takes the glass in both of her trembling hands and looks at him sadly. "Yes, I am... Only... I am not just looking for SOMEONE..."

Chapter 42

"What are you waiting for, Rosa? You know him!" The young woman walks back and forth in front of the door marked with the number 5. She chews on her cuticles nervously and glances down the corridor once in a while to make sure Carmelita can't see her. "Come on, what's the problem? You're just visiting a patient... Finding out how he's doing... And where he's from and what he's actually doing here... And why he won't speak to anyone but you... And ohhh, yeah... Whether he's on the run because he killed someone??!!" Even more upset than she was a minute before, she fidgets around, walking in tiny circles, and bites her hand. "Ouch!!" It was more painful than she expected. "Okay, that's it, you crazy woman! Do your job and stop being such a wimp! What did you swear to yourself when you were with Pablo? You have already gotten rid of Simon... Tsss... They should be happy together! They'll have a lot of babies, and make fun of you because you simply cannot stop talking to yourself like a crazy person, and you still live in this musty little apartment... in MEXICO!" Theatrically, just like the entire little scenario she just finished staging, she throws both hands over her head and sits down on them.

"Rosalía?"

Startled at hearing her name, she looks around her. But she sees no one anywhere. "Oh, Holy Mother of God!" Terrified, she covers her mouth with both hands and whispers softly through her fingers, "Hello? Pablo? Is that you?" Although she's afraid, Rosa looks up and down the corridor again, and then slowly lifts her face up towards the ceiling.

"Rosalía!" She hears the dull but clearly understandable voice again. "Rosalía, please!" The male voice seems to be very close and Rosalía's hands start shaking. "I, I'm here! Where are you?" Small beads of sweat pop out of her pores and she buttons up her white smock.

"I'm here inside! In the room! Rosalía, please, fast!"

It seems as if her internal horror can be felt in everything around her, like an icy shower of rain beating down on her mercilessly. Her skin turns even more pale and her mouth opens slowly. "I am about to lose it... I don't feel well... I am not feeling well at all... Help me! If there is a God, if there really is, then please, help me NOW!" She closes her eyes as if this would help clear up her vision. And in fact, she takes a deep breath and says a quick thank you to her yoga classes. She supports herself with one hand on the door and presses the other one against her chest. She once again hears the deep, clear male voice. "Rosalía? I'm in here! I can hear you! Why don't you help me?"

As if struck by lightning, Rosa opens her eyes and looks at the door she is touching. "Bob? Oh you stupid, stupid crazy idiot! BOB!" Without another thought, she pushes the door open and enters the room, which is as dark as night.

Chapter 43

Kenneth Conley, the young lawyer and professor, leafs through the file with care and concentration. The air inside the director's spacious office at the psychiatric clinic feels thick enough to cut. The tense, exhausted faces look at each other, trying to get and give hope to each other. Frank notices Susie's expression, showing that she's having a hard time trying to stay calm and wait. He winks mischievously at her, as if trying to shorten the waiting time. She takes this as encouragement to interrupt the stifling silence. "Tell me, Señor," she says in a sarcastic tone. "Who funds your institute... Or rather, your clinic?" As she asks this question, she gets up from the sofa and walks over to the window.

"What do you mean by that, Señora Conley?" He barely has time to ask this question before she interrupts. "Oh no, no, believe me, if I were Señora Conley…" But Frank interrupts her right away with a mischievous smile on his face. "La Señora doesn't like to talk about our status, I'm sure you understand… In America, it's all too complicated… But please, my sweetie pie, explain to the nice Señor Director what exactly you are interested in finding out."

Chuckling, Susie continues, "I wanted to know who pays for all this! The patients? The government? Private patrons? For example, who pays your salary?" She draws circles in the air with her forefinger, then points directly at the tiny bald Mexican man. The director looks first at Susie, and then, slightly irritated, at Frank, who raises his shoulders as if to say, "I don't know – I can't help you." Slightly embarrassed and blushing, the director steps away from Susie and clears his throat before trying to answer. "You know, Señora, here in Mexico, you have to figure out how to keep such a well-established clinic up to date. This is not possible without very good connections. I am a dedicated man and I have a very large network, which I specifically chose and take care of." Proud as a Boy Scout who has earned his first badge, he looks around the room to see who else is listening to him. When, to his disappointment, he sees that the only person paying him any attention is the rotund lady with a curious look on her face, he folds his hands together in front of his fat belly and addresses Tom. "You, Señor, surely know exactly what I mean by that!" The manager and agent shrugs his shoulders as if he has no idea what this is all about and then puts both his hands in his pockets without replying.

"But I know what you are talking about, Señor Director!" Ken, who appears to have reviewed the files thoroughly, approaches the small man, hands the papers back to him, and stands with his legs spread wide and his arms crossed in front of him.

Only his index finger rises and points at the papers. "You already know that you have no chance of getting away with THAT without a trace with the FBI involved!"

Chapter 44

"Rosalía? Are you here? Hello?... Please, help me!" Bob's pleading voice is clear and audible in the dark sickroom. Rosa's heart is beating so loudly in her chest that she feels as if it will burst. Her carotid artery now joins in, pulsating wildly. Her mouth dries up and swallowing turns into an anatomical challenge. Her hand feels around for the light switch and she pushes the switch up. The sudden light dazzles her eyes and she blinks as they adjust to the bright light. She covers her eyes for a second to help soften the sudden transition from complete darkness to blinding light. Slowly she begins to make things out in the room and her eyes move in the direction from which she heard Bob's voice. First her breath stops and then she covers her mouth with her hands, as if to suppress an uncontrolled scream.

"But, but… What is going on??... This is not possible! What is going on?!" She moves quickly over to the bed in the corner and stops abruptly next to it. "I am here! Bob, I'm here!" She speaks these words between heavy breaths, as if she had just been sprinting. "But… I don't understand… Bob, what is going on here? What did they do to you? What did YOU do?"

With hectic but gentle movements, she lifts the patient's heavy head and removes the bandage from his eyes. They start blinking immediately and he tries to hold them still in the glaring light. His pupils try to focus and his irises do their best to provide support. Rosalía now also helps by shading his eyes with her hands. As soon as the dancing blue eyes calm down, the still worried physiotherapist puts both of her hands on the patient, who is tied up to the bed. "Bob, can I untie you now? Don't do anything stupid, comprendes? I have really had too much happen to me today…"

"Rosalía, I won't do anything to you!" answers Bob, confused. "You're the only person I have! Help me! Please!"

The renewed genuine confusion in his voice convinces the angel in white to untie the bands holding his hands tightly to the bedposts. First she frees one hand, then walks around the bed to untie the other also. Then she notices something under the sheet.

"But, what the heck..?"

Chapter 45

"FBI? What does the FBI want with me? We are here in Mexico! We are not interested in

171

the opinion of your F... B... I..., Señor Lawyer!" The small director's voice suddenly stops sounding polite and obliging. His piercing gaze does not turn away from Ken as he emphasizes the syllables loudly and sarcastically. But Ken does not let this bother him in any way and directs his next words to Linda and Frank. "Simon is here!" Linda jumps up immediately and starts to walk towards the door, but Frank holds her back. "Wait, wait, I want to hear the whole story first." He looks at Ken again. "Go on."

But before Ken can answer, the Mexican man interrupts him. "First of all, I want to know if this will go smoothly for ME and of course for my institute as well! As we discussed, no attention, no police, no TV! And of course, the payment we agreed on!?" He looks questioningly at Tom while placing both hands protectively on the files, as if they were the Holy Grail. Tom looks at Ken, shaking his head questioningly. "Is this pile of paper worth anything at all?"

"Not a single peso! Wait, what am I saying? Not a single centavo!" replies the young lawyer from New York. "And yet, we are not inhuman and we could think about coming up with something in payment for the hint that Simon and Mirjam are here..." His gaze wanders from his father to Linda, who suddenly turns pale, swallows loudly and tries to find her voice. "Mirjam too?" she asks slowly, in a barely audible voice. "Is there also anything about Roberto in there?"

All eyes are now tensely focused on Ken, who surprisingly shrugs his shoulders. "I can't say. At least, he's not mentioned by name. There... There was apparently an accident that Simon was involved in... And..."

"An accident?" Frank's astonishment speaks for everyone connected with him and he adds, "What does this have to do with his job application here? This makes no sense!"

"Unfortunately, that is the ONLY thing that makes sense, Dad!" Ken looks sadly at Linda before he continues speaking. "Because he explains the… His adopted paternity of Mirjam…"

Chapter 46

Rosalía takes a long look at the package in her hands and then carefully puts it back on the bed. "What is there? What did you see? What was under the covers? Rosalía?" The still tied-up patient excitedly asks one question after another. The physiotherapist stops on the other side of the bed and unties the second band from the patient's wrist. "A package, Bob, it's a package." She picks it up again and sits down at the foot of the bed. Bob rubs his wrists and forehead. "You must help me, Rosa. I am being wronged!"

The exhausted Mexican woman slowly looks into Bob's injured eyes and says, "Then there are now two of us in the Heaven for the Unjustly Treated!" She places the package in the middle of the bed, on top of the still lame legs of her favorite patient, and knocks loudly on it with one hand. "Where should we start?" She clears her throat and continues drumming her fingers on the box. "Why are you tied up here in the dark? Or… What is in this package? Or… How can we find out who it's from? …Or do you not know the answers to those questions?" She notices her sarcastic undertone herself before he can answer, and adds quickly, "I shouldn't have said it like that… Lo siento…! But you must understand, Bob, we are in a psychiatric hospital here… A lunatic asylum… Una hacienda de LOCOS!" She tries to add more weight to her statement by making the typical "crazy" hand gesture.

"I know… And that's precisely why I am HERE!" The confused patient raises both of his arms in the air. "Please, Rosa, listen to me! We can't let any more time pass by. My daughter is in danger!"

Puzzled and visibly irritated, Rosa looks at him. "Your daughter? I didn't know…" But she is interrupted by a knock at the door.

"Todo bien?" They hear Carmen call out. Rosa replies quickly. "Todo bien!" As if that would prevent the curious nurse from entering. But it appears to have worked because they hear footsteps walking away from the door. Rosa exhales the breath she has been holding and turns back to Bob. "You never told me you have children!"

Chapter 47

"I've had enough! I do not like your country or your loony bins and I really cannot stand you personally!" Susie shouts these words at the director and emphasizes them with wild hand gestures. She goes over to the door, puts her hand on the doorknob and looks at Frank and Ken. "Gentlemen, please excuse me. The lady must stand up for decent Americans! All of this here," and she draws a circle in the air with her index finger, then continues, "looks like an ancient steam locomotive!" She holds up her hand, palm outward. "Alright, I can figure things out myself! If I'm not back in ten minutes, it means I've been kidnapped and sold to a bullfighter! If everyone here looks like that one over there," and she points her head towards the director and continues, "then I'm a Victoria's Secret model in this country!" She opens the door to leave, but Linda stops her by speaking. "Wait, Susie, I'll go with you."

Outside in the waiting room, Susie puts her hand on Linda's arm. "You do realize that I don't have to go to the potty, right, sweetie?" She looks questioningly into Linda's dull eyes.

"I knew immediately by your expression! And believe me, Frank and Ken also saw through us! Let's go!" With that, they go over to the elevator and press the button to go to the next floor down. "I would suggest one floor at a time... What do we have here?... No idea... Everything's in Spanish... Of course... Tsss..." Susie throws both hands theatrically in the air and rolls her eyes behind her small reading glasses, which are attached to the traditional gold chain around her neck. She looks questioningly at Linda. "From the top to the bottom or do we want to work our way up?" The Swiss woman pushes hard on the lowest button, looks at Susie and replies, "Good things come from above! But the opposite seems to be true here!" Susie's eyes sparkle and she winks one of them. "CLEVER girl!"

The shaky elevator seems to take an eternity to get down to the first floor of the building. The two women watch the display indicating the floors and stay silent at first. Both are absorbed in their own thoughts and are considering the next possible steps. As if having the same thought simultaneously, they look at each other and Linda is the first to ask a not insignificant question. "And what if we actually see him?"

"I'll scratch his eyes out!" Susie completes the thought out loud.

Chapter 48

The physiotherapist's horrified, chalk-white face appears to be frozen. Only her large dark eyes show any emotion as her black eyelashes move up and down. After a few seconds that feel like an eternity, she clears her throat, swallows loudly and tries to formulate a reasonable sentence. But the only sound that can get past her vocal cords is a quiet whimper.

"I know it all sounds unimaginable and crazy, but please... PLEASE... Rosalía... Rosa... You must believe me! Help me! Help us! Mirjam and me! She... She has already lost her mom... Help me so that she can at least have her father... Or at least what's left of him...!"

Rosalía clears her throat again as a bit of animation slowly return to her face. She puts her ice cold, trembling hand on the package that is still lying between them and speaks again. "I... I don't know, Bob... Roberto... To me, all of this sounds like a terrible horrible horror movie!... I would never watch a movie like that... Do you understand?... Well, actually... I wouldn't even dream of reading a book like that! This is inhuman… This… This is crazy! LOCO!! It's CRAZY!!!" Her complexion changes slowly from chalk-white to purple. Blotches appear on her neck and her carotid artery, which is now visible, begins throbbing dangerously. She slowly gets up from the bed and Bob's face tries to follow the noises of her movements.

"Rosa! Please! I know! I was… I AM a monster… A cowardly idiot… But please try to understand…" He stretches his hands pleadingly towards her.

"Understand??!! UNDERSTAND??!! I am supposed to TRY TO UNDERSTAND!!??" Her now extremely loud words reverberate in the small sterile room like thunder inside a mountain cave. "You are an ANIMAL! An insane, selfish, destructive, insensitive and brutal animal! Someone should slaughter you! Yes, exactly! I should take you to the slaughterhouse! OHHHH and mierda… Dios mio! You have no idea what

Mexican butchers are like! Hold on! A Muslim butcher! Even better! He would let you bleed out and...!" In a matter of seconds, Rosalía has gotten into a rage that even she has never known was inside of her. She looks around the room, looking for a way out of this terrible scene, when the door opens as if by magic. She bites her lower lip, takes a deep breath, and looks with surprise, frowning at the faces that appear in the doorway.

Chapter 49

The door of the old elevator opens slowly and the two women step hesitantly out into the gloomy corridor. Only one flickering lightbulb offers a bit of light and icy cold air wafts by them. Linda wraps her hands around her upper arms for warmth and protection within her own embrace. Susie lets her glasses dangle on their chain and squints down the empty corridor. "Hmm… I wonder if this is the disposal unit?"

"Susan!" Linda's seriously horrified voice does nothing to stop her sarcastic companion. "Look around you! Darkness, the optimal temperature… I am certain that the forgotten or hopeless are lying somewhere around here! Or do you think a madhouse also holds wakes for the dead?" Curious, she walks towards a door and starts to open it. But Linda is quicker and jumps between Susie and the unaired secret. "No, absolutely not! I don't know, Susie, but I don't think this is right… What are we thinking?! Look around! What are we doing here? Do we really want to open EVERY door we pass? What if there really is someone here? Dead or alive?"

"Then… Then… We'll wave! I don't know either, but the money-hungry, pot-bellied pig upstairs was driving me crazy! I would rather deal with absolutely crazy people or completely

mute people! Anything would be better than…"
Her agitated words are interrupted by a door
opening further down the corridor. Both women
look in that direction, terrified and anxious. A
man wearing jeans and a T-shirt holds the door
open while two other men, also dressed
casually, come out of the room holding a long
wooden box. Susie whispers, "So a wake for the
dead after all… I wonder if he died willingly."

Linda makes a horrified sound, which is
heard by the three people at the other end of the
corridor. The man with nothing in his hands calls
out incomprehensible words in Spanish. "I think
he doesn't want us to be here. They have
something to hide, I'm telling you!" While Susie
continues to watch the three men curiously,
Linda tries to push her towards the elevator.
"Let's get out of here. I don't like this situation!"
She presses the small button on the wall and
then notices the door behind her, which reflects
the image of a staircase. "Come on, we'll take

the stairs! That ancient shaking box will take too long!"

Susie's loud breathing sounds like repeated blasts of thunder in the staircase. "Do you want to put me in a wooden box also? What is going on here? WE are not on the run! THEY are!" She stops and holds on to the railing with both hands. "I don't even want to know what kind of disgusting hands have touched this!" She snorts loudly. But then she hears Linda opening a door a bit further up the stairs, talking to someone.

Chapter 50

"What are you doing here, Rosalía?" With one eyebrow raised, the psychiatrist who has just entered the room looks at the physiotherapist standing at the other end of the room. Next to him stands the grinning nurse, holding a small tray in her hand. "You should not be here and you know it!" Slowly he walks towards Rosalía after holding the door open for the gum-chewing witch.

"What? Why not? Since when am I not allowed or am I now FORBIDDEN to visit my patients?" Her eagle eyes follow the tray, which is being carried towards Bob. Jeff, the American Psycho, as they all call him, turns to face her, but she refuses to let her view be blocked.

"What kinds of medications are these? I don't know anything about medications! Hey, that's not in his medical records!" She tries to walk towards the bed but is held back gently by the plumber with a medical doctor title on his name tag. "Just routine medications to calm him down. We heard loud voices, which is completely understandable and normal."

Rosa pushes past her colleague, walks around the bed to Carmelita and extends her open hand. "Then give them to me! I was the one who was shouting! So these medications are for me! I need a LOT of calming down. If anyone, YOU should know that, right Carmelita?" She waves her outstretched hand, at the same time putting the other one in her pocket. She feels the rolled-up piece of paper she put there earlier in the morning. Before she can even think about whether the action she is about to take really makes sense, she takes the small rolled up piece of paper out and holds it up in the air. "You can have this in exchange!"

"Wait, wait!" the drug prescriber says. "Nothing will be exchanged here! What is that anyway?! Show me, Rosa!" He walks quickly over to Rosa's upraised hand and tries to take the rolled up piece of paper from her. But the clever woman is faster and puts both of her hands and the piece of paper back in her pockets. "Nothing to you, Jeff, but EXTREMELY interesting to your drug dealer here! Tell me, do you have absolutely no pride in your duties as a nurse? Do you even know what kinds of pills you are trying to give him? Just take a look at him! He is calm! He isn't moving. He isn't even talking to either of you! What is going on in this lowlife institution anyway?!"

Chapter 51

"Muchas gracias, Señorita!" Linda slams the door closed behind her and jumps over to Susie excitedly. "I did it, I really did, Susie!" Out of breath, not only from jumping, but from extreme nervousness, she can barely get those few words out. Linda is still gasping for breath and Susie looks at her. "What did you do? Ask Santa Claus to come visit me with his reindeer and sleigh? Seriously, Linda, I am writing my will here!" She reaches for Linda's hand and places it on her plump breast where her heart is located. "Feel it! Even though there's a lot of flesh in front of it, you can feel my heart pounding. I am certain it's going to explode any second now!" Despite the visibly exhausted her friend gives her, Linda pays no attention to her. "I did it! I simply asked for Simon Zimmermann. Just as if it were the most natural thing in the world!"

Slowly, step by step, the two women walk down the stairs in silence. "I'm really sorry, sweetie with the sexy butt, but I must save my last bit of strength for that scoundrel so I can put him in a chokehold before the little Mexican policemen spoil all my fun!" Susie concentrates on keeping one hand on the railing to prevent herself from stumbling because she can't see the steps below her large belly. "I think I could stand to lose a pound or two! Not too many all at once. I've heard that's not good for your skin!" Linda smiles politely and replies, "I'm going to spoil your fun with the chokehold now... Simon is almost two meters tall... I can feel my heart pounding in my chest, Susie... Do you think Frank is already on the way?"

They open the heavy staircase door and enter the empty corridor from which they came. Without speaking, they cross it, push the elevator button and wait tensely. After a few minutes, the elevator door opens. Susie can't hold back a surprised "Caramba!"

A small, strikingly attractive Mexican woman is standing inside the ancient elevator, apparently interrupted in the middle of an excited monologue. "Oh, lo siento!" She is clearly embarrassed to have been caught by the two women. With one hand, she grabs her smooth ponytail and looks at the floor, ashamed. She walks between the two women, but after a few short steps, she turns around and asks in quick Spanish, "Have you lost your way?"

Chapter 52

With her shoulders slumped and a disappointed look on her face, Rosalía stands in the open doorway and looks into the empty room. "You're already gone, Pablo... I am sorry that I missed you... You would not believe what's going on here! But you know what? This is also my last day at this hell hole! I am fed up – it's just a bit too crazy for me! What do I say, at least a hundred million steps to go! If I only knew what I am supposed to do next!" She looks down the poorly lit corridor and puts both hands in her pockets, one of them touching the rolled-up piece of paper. She takes it out and slowly unfolds it. Her eyes look at it, but she doesn't read it. Instead, she slowly squints her eyes. Her gaze wanders over to the elevator and she tilts her head sideways. "Wait... What did those two women just say?" She crumples up the piece of paper that was just neatly rolled up, quickly puts it back in her pocket, and walks over to the elevator with ever-quickening steps. She hears the elevator rattling and flails her hand. "Mierda! Mierda! Mierda!" She looks behind her and goes down the corridor to the fire escape.

"Go, go, go!" Light-footed, she takes two steps at a time up to the second floor. "Ahh... You have definitely neglected cardio!... Uhhh... Ok... You've only reached first gear... Just one more floor, Rosa! Come on!" Out of breath, she reaches the third floor, leans against the door and takes two deep breaths. "Physio... They said they were going to physiotherapy! That is MY department! So they definitely want to go see me! Now stay calm... She sounded very American... Hmm and she could be a director... At least that's what she looks like... Or a professor... Oh dios mio!!! Can it actually be true that my wish is going to come true on THIS kind of day? I never even expected that they would show up here in person! Oh heavens!!! I

REALLY hope they don't run into the Señor Director! Mierda! He will kill me on the spot!"

She hops back and forth on the landing, loosening her arms as if preparing to fight. She relaxes her shoulders, stretches her neck, breathes deeply in and out, puts her hand on the doorknob, and opens the heavy barrier between herself and her department. She steps into the corridor and looks straight into the dark eyes of the younger of the two women she met in the basement a few minutes ago.

Chapter 53

"Holy margarita!!! If the men were just half as attractive as this little woman, this would be the Promised Land! That must have been a goddess, Linda! Have you ever seen anything like that live? Seriously now! I mean, Frank is certainly used to that, but I only see things like that in my little cubicle on the screen! What do you think – is she a doctor? She had a smock on… Hmm… Is she single? We should show Ken to her…!" Susie's excited chatter has made the bumpy elevator ride seem shorter and Linda silently thanks her for changing her mind. Even though she has only actually listened to about half of what Susie is saying, she has to admit that the sight of that small Mexican woman was striking. After just a few more minutes, the elevator stops and the door to the third floor corridor opens.

"Say, my lovely, what did you ask and who did you ask? Do you see?! I knew it – sports simply are not good for me! Seriously! I have tried so many times but every time, I get the same side effects. I forget everything! It's true – I simply cannot concentrate after extreme physical effort. No, I really should not overdo it like that anymore. I don't even know what we're doing here! Isn't that terrible?" With her hands positioned on her bulging hips, Susie looks down

194

the corridor, lost. "At least here it looks more decent and lively than in the filthy basement!" Her index finger supports this statement by pointing to the reasonably clean floor.

"I simply asked for Simon Zimmermann..." Linda replies as she looks around a bit nervously. She walks slowly in one direction along the corridor. "The lady on the first floor knew immediately who I was looking for and said that he's working in the Physiotherapy department, here on the third floor. Strange, actually... What is he doing in the Physiotherapy department? He doesn't know anything about physiotherapy!" She continues walking aimlessly in the same direction and resumes speaking. "So let's go! I would suggest walking up and down the corridor once. As if we were visiting someone. And if someone comes, we'll just ask about him again. What do you think, Susie?" She turns around, but Susan Manders is no longer behind her.

"Susie?" Astonished, she looks around. No, not a trace of the blabbermouth. "This can't be! Susan!" Linda raises both hands in the air, then places them on her hips and looks down the silent, empty corridor.

Chapter 54

"Buenos días, Señora. We just met down there." Rosalía nervously waves one hand in the air, while the other strokes her smooth-combed hair a little shakily. "I'm sorry I was a bit absent and so rude. What can I do for you? Are you looking for someone specific here in the Physiotherapy department?" Curious, the small Mexican woman looks into the now even more confused eyes of the visitor in front of her, who frowns slightly and then looks back down the empty corridor. "Yes, um... Actually, I'm looking for two people... Did you see the lady I was with when I met you down there?" She turns to look again at Rosa. "By the way, you were wicked quick!"

Easily embarrassed, Rosa looks down at the floor and smiles. "Yes, if need be, I can be very fast." She steps into the middle of the corridor and points to the elevator. "You just rode up together. Where could she be?" She points her hand around her. "Or did I just misunderstand you? It's often harder to communicate with someone who also has an accent, right? Where are you from, if I may ask?" Secretly, Rosa now hopes to hear the name of the land of her dreams, even if she remembers the Scottish dialect differently from the films and documentaries. But there are probably many dialects there, and she has definitely not heard all of them by far, but she can hardly wait.

"Pardon me?" Still confused by Susie's sudden disappearance, Linda looks at the beautiful woman right in front of her. "Yes, I don't know either. She was just here! I just turned away and thought aloud... But it cannot be! Susie?!" Once again, she calls out the name of her vanished friend, this time a little louder and more clearly. "Susie, this is not funny!" She goes past the small physiotherapist and over to the first door. She starts to open it, but Rosa stops her and waves at it. "That's just the supply closet. Let's try the next one. That's the staff room. Maybe she was thirsty or hungry. There are drinks and food, although it's only for employees." As she speaks, she goes to the next door and opens it. Before she can enter, Linda scurries past her: "Susan? Are you here?"

Chapter 55

"Your ladies do not seem to have found the restroom, Señor!" The small fat Mexican man walks towards the door of his office as if he can see through it. Frank slowly gets up from the leather sofa, gives his son a meaningful look and replies to the nervous director in a soft tone of voice. "No, it does not look that way and I think we should help them look, since it's clear we cannot get any further here. I assume that you will give us free access to your... Well, how can I put it nicely... Your institution? Or should we continue with Plan B?"

"Plan B? What's Plan B?" Even more nervous than before, the small guy walks over to his desk in just a few small steps and opens a drawer, carefully placing the file inside of it. Ken starts speaking. "We call the FBI and demand extradition of a fugitive and also throw you to the lions to eat because of falsification of American STATE documents, which you were clearly aware of... You KNOWINGLY helped a fugitive!"

The sleazy director's laugh sounds so loud that it startles the three other people in the room. "The FBI!?... That's a good one!

Gentlemen, as I already mentioned, this is Mexican soil on which you stand, stamping your feet! YOUR FBI will give me protection, yes, even support me! No matter how famous you are, Mr. CONLEY!" He emphasizes the name with a derogatory undertone. "In this matter, the FBI is on my side! Comprendes?"

Tom walks over to the director's desk and looks directly into the excited man's eyes. "Why should the FBI be on your side? What's going on here?"

"Well, YOU are not the only one looking for someone in my clinic!" This is his response, which he accompanies with an arrogant look and confidence in his victory.

"The FBI has informed US! Because they just cannot do anything here... What's going on here? Who else is still being searched for in your CLINIC?" The otherwise very organized and controlled manager hisses his words across the desk. "Whatever you want to assume, my little friend, it was definitely not the FBI!"

Chapter 56

The surprisingly spacious staff room is also deserted. Linda wonders to herself first, and then asks the question out loud. "Are there not very many patients here or is it usually this quiet? I haven't seen anyone." She looks questioningly into the beautiful, excited sparkling eyes of her new companion and wonders how she can ask for Simon without having to give a lot of details. She and Susie have actually not given much thought to this plan. Where are Frank and Ken? Everything takes too long. She wants to get away from here, out of Mexico. She wants to have Roberto, and above all Mirjam, back. Even her own thoughts are playing a joke on her. Actually, she just wants Mirjam back. She doubts very much if she could ever forgive

Roberto for leaving her alone and doing this to her.

"Señorita!? Is everything okay?" The gentle touch of the person next to her yanks her out of her thoughts. "It helps if you think things through out loud! Then maybe I can help you! Well, not everything that I think about out loud helps me. It happens to me from time to time, but there have been moments when it was quite good. I assume that you didn't hear my answer just now? I know that feeling all too well." Rosalía's agitated ranting seems to irritate Linda. She turns on her heel and heads back down the corridor.

"Ok, we are looking for Susan. Your friend? Boss? Work colleague?" Rosa continues asking questions as she walks in front of Linda down the corridor to the next door. "This is my treatment room. No one should be in here now." Nevertheless, she opens the door and holds it open so that Linda can see the empty room for herself and also see that Rosa's statement is true.

Linda looks back into the beautiful eyes of the petite and visibly fit young woman in front of her. "Do you have children?" Her eyes look down at the name tag on the white coat, then she politely adds, "Rosalía?"

"These clever Scots." Rosa thinks and has to pull herself together tightly to stop herself from saying these thoughts out loud. She bites her lower lip for a fraction of a second and thinks, "Aha, a trick question in a casual introductory conversation. So... This Susan has most likely not disappeared at all, and they want to test me... You can try, Señorita!'

Chapter 57

Confident of their victory and with suppressed grins, the three visitors step out of the director's office and pass by the receptionist. In the big room behind them, the little Mexican sits in his leather chair and looks up in dismay at the empty wooden desk in front of him. The three amigos politely say goodbye to the secretary and Tom lays a bundle of pesos on her desk. "You can give that to your boss in there when you take him a valium or a tequila. He could certainly use something!" He then slaps the desk with his hand and winks at her.

"Tom, the creaky old elevator is here!" Frank stands in the open elevator door and waves his agent over.

"Third floor, right? Physiotherapy intern! Tsss... If he's smart, he probably found shelter in the operating rooms, where everyone is unconscious or lying half dead on the table.

Anyone would be able to recognize him here! That's also what our oh-so-smart director did!" All three men laugh at Frank's statement, and while Ken presses the button for the third floor, he adds, "Besides, he's also looking for someone... Or..." A mysterious look appears on his face as he looks at Frank and Tom. "He must have someone under surveillance..."

"What do you mean? What is actually written in this mysterious file that the nasty little hack wanted to use to earn his retirement?" Frank puts both hands in his pockets after opening the top button of his shirt. Small beads of sweat appear on his temples and he exhales a full blast of air, as if that would help him cool off. All four eyes are now directed at the lively attorney.

"This Simon Zimmermann applied here as an intern to pursue a new path in medicine and life. In his cover letter, he describes a tragic accident in which his best friend and his wife were killed. The woman had been very pregnant, but only the baby was able to be saved, which he then of course adopted. In order to leave behind this tragic experience, he has decided to make a fresh start with his child here in Mexico." Ken raises his eyebrows, leans his head slightly to the side and clicks his tongue before continuing. "However, the oh-so-clever guy has made a mistake, which the little blowhard upstairs obviously did not even notice..."

Chapter 58

"Me? Children?! Dios mío, no, no Señora... What was your name?" Rosa extends her hand for the belated introduction, noting that the woman in front of her has a strikingly flat chest, too flat for the normal female anatomy, and she wonders why, in these times, she isn't wearing a padded bra... Is she doing it on purpose? Linda notices that Rosa is staring too long at her body, grasps the hand held out to her and answers, "My name is Linda. And yes, I had breast cancer." Ashamed at being caught staring, the beautiful face of the physiotherapist turns slightly red and she whispers. "Lo siento mucho, Señora. I'm sorry. Are you alright? I mean, did this happen a long time ago?" She now looks into Linda's eyes, medical interest replacing her confusion, and is surprised with an unexpected counter question. "Do you know Simon?"

"Excuse me?" Not yet aware of the change in topic and still focused on Linda's fate, Rosalía looks dumbfounded at the face in front of her. She must have misunderstood. This cannot be. What would Simon have to do with her application in Scotland? He doesn't know anything about it... Or does he?

"Do you know a Simon? Simon Zimmermann. I was told that he works in this department as an intern." Linda's serious, almost obtrusive look hits the sensitive Mexican woman like a tornado.

Rosa's knees start to collapse, her pulse starts to quicken, her palms start getting wet and she feels her fingers swelling slowly into small chipolata sausages. Her saliva dries slowly, like a puddle on hot asphalt. She tries to focus her eyes, but her vision is slowly fading. The extremely clear face of the young woman in front of her disappears into a tunnel-like tube. She understands that the woman is speaking to her, but her voice sounds like a broken tape that has been rewound too many times and her words now sound like a whale song. She feels a hard, aching blow to her head and tries to understand why she can now see the tiles of the floor of the corridor up close.

Chapter 59

"Third floor. When I get that little hack between my fingers!" Frank clenches his fists so hard that the knuckles gleam white through his skin. "Then you behave and we're only going to talk to him for now. He's only going to shit himself if he sees all three of us. We still need him, at least until we know where Mirjam is. After that, he's all yours." Tom holds his raised hand in front of Frank's chest, which moves violently up and down.

"Just you two. I'm going to the nurse's station in the meantime. We can't waste any more time. Susie and Linda are still here somewhere! Didn't even one of them text you, Dad? "Ken stands in the elevator doorway, holding it open for the other two. As Frank pulls his Blackberry out of his pocket, he takes two big steps down the corridor.

"Linda!? What is going on...!?" Frank sees Linda kneeling, bent over a motionless body, and runs to her, followed by Tom and Ken.

"What happened? Who is this? And where is Susie?" He asks one question after the other as he kneels down to get closer to the petite person lying on the ground and instinctively feels her carotid artery.

Linda has a look of horror on her chalk-white face and she shakes her head: "I don't know what happened. She... She was going to look for Susie with me and... And... When I asked her about Simon, she just fell down... Her eyes rolled back and she was out... Rosalía. She said her name is Rosalía. I have no idea... And Susie... She just disappeared... Disappeared... From one second to the next! This is a madhouse here! I want to leave! I want to find Miriam! I cannot stand it anymore! Enough! Enough! Simply enough now!!" Her increasingly loud and hysterical voice resounds in the corridor like thunder followed by a thunderstorm.

Ken quickly grabs her shoulders, helps her to her feet and hugs her. "Shh.. shh... We'll get there soon! I promise! Everything will be fine!" Then he turns to his father. "Quick, let's get them to the fourth floor. Go, fast!" As he finishes giving instructions to his father, he lifts the unconscious woman and hurries with her to the fire escape: "Tom, open it! That crappy elevator will take too long! God, this little one is heavy! She certainly didn't look this heavy at first glance! "

Chapter 60

Never in her life has she imagined it to be so beautiful! She sits down on a large stone that sits proudly next to the river, takes off her hiking boots and rolls her jeans up to her knees. Slowly she dips her toes into the refreshing cool water of the mountain stream and closes her eyes. She listens to the flowing stream, the otherwise endless silence and hears a seagull screech. Carefully, she opens one eye after another, so as not to lose the calm inside her head. Her dark, sparkling eyes sweep with pleasure over the vastness of the enticing view. Her highlands! Her Scottish Highlands! She did it, she is here.

Rosalía pulls the band out of her hair with one hand and lets her wild curls dance in the wind. From afar, she hears the hoofs of a galloping horse. The strong creature seems to be coming closer to her because the hoofbeats are getting louder and clearer. She turns her head and sees a black horse and rider approaching. She gets up off the stone, while the rider commands his horse to walk, approaching at a slower pace in her direction. The warm sun behind him does not let her see his face, but she can see his big strong shoulders in his silhouette. He stops his horse right next to her and puts out his hand to help her mount.

"Rosalia? Rosa? Can I call you Rosa?" She hears his deep voice ask. Her name sounds like a love poem coming out of his mouth and his voice gives her goose bumps. He can call her whatever he wants! "Rosalía, can you hear me??" She reaches to take the hand he is holding out to her and replies, "You have the most beautiful voice I have ever heard! And you can call me whatever you want! Just take me away from here! Take me with you!" She tries again to grab his hand and then feels it, warm, strong and yet gentle in her own. He squeezes her hand tenderly and gently, as if he doesn't want to hurt her, as if he has just been given the most delicate gift he has ever received.

"Oh, that's very nice of you, thank you, Rosa! I will see what I can do. Would you like to try and open your eyes first?"

Chapter 61

"But, how can this be? How is this supposed to work? This simply cannot be!" Frank looks frantically back and forth between Linda and Tom. "She can't have just dissolved in thin air, Tom!" As if his agent always has the right answer to his questions, Frank looks at him, holding his hands together as if in prayer in front of his chest. The manager takes his mobile phone out of his pocket and while he is typing on it, he asks, "Did you check your messages?"

"Right! I was just going to do that when we found you with the little one on the floor." He makes this remark to Linda, who leans her pale head against the wall behind her, her eyes closed, her arms in a defensive position. "The little one's name is Rosalía. I can't shake the feeling that she knows something. We met her in the basement while we were on our way to the Physiotherapy department. She asked us where we wanted to go. But she initially responded as if she were extremely uninterested, as if she were mentally somewhere else... And she definitely was because we caught her in the act of talking to herself. But then..." Linda lifts her head away from the wall and opens her eyes. "But then she came after us. Imagine, she ran up the four floors to intercept us. That's weird... Or do you think she's crazy? She did not seem crazy at all..." Linda is interrupted in her monologue of thoughts she's speaking out loud by loud cursing from Frank.

"Good Lord!!!" With anger, followed by horror in his eyes, he looks from his BlackBerry first to Linda, then to Tom. He turns the screen of his phone in Tom's direction. At first he says nothing, but then shows the screen to Linda as well, saying quietly, "He has Susie!"

Tom takes Conley's Blackberry out of his hand and reads aloud, so that Linda can hear the message at the same time. "Your lady is fine and will stay that way. I'm just asking you to let me go. I know that Jasmine is alive and looking for her baby. She is fine, too. I will tell you where she is if you promise not to inform the police. Then I'll have Susan wait for you with the baby. Give me your word, Conley. I know you are a man of honor! And the following words are for Jasmine." Tom turns the screen to Jasmine, who stares at it with horrified eyes, claps her hands over her mouth and sends out a painful cry along the corridor.

Chapter 62

Why should she open her eyes? Her eyes are open anyway and she... Oh... No... Please no!! Rosalía understands... She understands and is ashamed to the bone. Through the small slits of her almost closed eyes, tears slowly escape and search for a way down her soft pink cheeks. She presses her lips and the hand, which she is still holding with her own, gently together. She has to convince herself of this repeat faux pas.

"Do not cry, Rosa! I'm sorry... Oh no, I'm so sorry... I pulled you out of a dream, didn't I?" The wonderful voice of her Highlander, who has just saved her, strikes softly at her eardrums like a tender feather. She keeps her eyes closed and her lips pressed together but nods yes to his question.

"I will bring you a glass of water. Wait, all I have to do is walk around your bed. There's a bottle over there." The big, yet tender hand delicately peels itself out of Rosa's claws and she feels him rising from the bed. She dares to open one eye slightly to spy on her Highlander on horseback in reality, without him noticing.

His strong physique clearly shows signs of sports activities. His broad shoulders are packed into a polo shirt, his slim hips in perfectly fitting jeans, held up with a wide leather belt. He walks casually, but with precise movements. Strong arms protrude from the short sleeves of his shirt and a watch with a leather strap adorns his wrist. As his body goes around the bed, she closes her eye again and is again robbed of the sight of his face. She can hear him handling the glass bottle next to her and she feels his breath lightly caressing her as he sits down on her bed again.

"Should I raise your head so you can drink?" The Scottish voice with an American accent speaks to her. Her thoughts are playing ping-pong and she cannot decide which side should win. A hint of peppermint caresses her face and she feels a searching hand trying to lift her head. "Here, it has a drinking straw. Wait, all you have to do is open your mouth. Then you'll feel better." Her lips touch the cool plastic and she opens her mouth to drink, just as she was instructed.

"Now don't act even stupider than you already are! Open your eyes. Go on, do it! He will think you are a total idiot! Go on!"

She slowly opens her eyes, blinks a few times to get used to the blinding light, and says softly, "Gracias." She then looks directly into the eyes in front of her. Her blood starts to freeze, her vocal cords turn into long rubber bands and her heart starts beating loudly.

.

Chapter 63

Like a hunted deer in the woods, Linda sprints to the next door on the opposite side of the corridor and flings it open. She runs inside but comes out of the door immediately afterwards. "Linda! What are you doing there? What's written here! "Frank holds his Blackberry in the air and looks at Tom with raised shoulders and a questioning look on his face.

"He is here! He has to be here! He's alive!" Screaming these words hysterically, Linda tries to open the next door at the same time as someone else opens it from the other side and a malicious-looking nurse blocks her way.

"Caramba! Qué pasa aquí?" She snaps at Linda, continuing to chew her gum and throwing her hands theatrically into the air.

Frank and Tom race over to stand next to Linda and Frank holds his hand apologetically between the two women. With her chewing gum visibly lying on her lower jaw, the fancy hair-styled nurse stares at him. "Pero... Santa Lucía...!!" She waves both of her hands in front of her still open mouth and lets out a sort of squeaking sound.

"Hi! Excuse me, we were too loud! We just had a..." Frank tries to explain the inexplicable situation with a handshake as the nurse catches one of his hands in the air, holds it close to her between her two hands, and pulls him over to her. She blinks at him with glowing eyes, stares at him and places his hand on her overly made-up cheek. "Oh mi madre... This is not a dream... Oh heavens... He is actually... Flesh and blood!"

Linda steps from one foot to the other, looks around nervously down the corridor, and cannot stand it one second longer – the way Frank is recognized and adored is driving her nuts. "Please, help us, where is Roberto?!" Desperately, she looks at the still amazed Mexican woman, who doesn't even glance at her. Still fixated on Conley and yet torn from her reveries, she replies, "No conozco Roberto."

Chapter 64

"Rosa? May I still call you that?" The Highlander on horseback, who has turned into flesh and blood, is still sitting on her bed, holding a glass with a drinking straw in one hand, and the other lying gently on her forearm. She tries to nod her head, but she doesn't know if he really asked her. She looks into those lovely eyes, into his handsome face, and gazes at his strong cheekbones, his full lips, and follows the angular line of his nose, then lets her eyes wander over his shoulders to his chest.

"My name is Kenneth Conley. But please call me Ken." As he introduces himself politely, with the gesture of a gentleman, placing one hand on his chest, Rosalía imagines what she looks like. At the thought of this, she starts to feel sick to her stomach. But she immediately thinks about how unsuitable vomiting would be now. What did Mamá always warn her about?

"Beware, my love, your thoughts will come true..."

***

"Ohhh, ok!... All right! Exactly... Just get it out!... That's good... All right... Don't cry... It's all right... This can happen after a person faints... You're doing fine... Don't cry, Rosa... Let it out..." After Ken has responded heroically and is standing on his feet in a flash next to the disaster in the bed, he caresses the still choking woman gently on her bent over back.

"Everything out? Or is more coming?" He bends down next to her and she could not feel more ashamed. She wishes a tornado would appear right here, a big black hole in front of her that would swallow her up and take her out of this scene. She cannot stop crying and she does not dare lift her head to look at the man of her dreams. She feels his warm hand on her back and looks at her vomit on the bed in front of her.

Chapter 65

"Gracias, Señorita!" These are the first and only words that Frank can say to the nurse because Tom interrupts and, in perfect Spanish, addresses the female fan. "Excuse us for causing a ruckus at your station, but we are urgently looking for two – wait, no, what am I saying – three people here at the clinic. If you'd like, we will gladly take a picture of you with Frank and he will also autograph something. But please, help us find our way in this labyrinth!" He claps his hands together in front of his chest and then discards this attitude immediately.

After several photos of the two have been taken in an exaggerated session, the unrestrained employee takes a marker from her smock, opens the top three buttons and passes the marker to Frank. She seductively holds her coat open, pushes her breasts out in the white lace bra, and says in broken English, "Please,

Señor Frank, write something nice on here, for Carmelita!"

Linda's horrified look at Tom is answered with a raised eyebrow and a soft click of his tongue. He walks the few steps over to her and whispers softly, "That's why I should become an actor. Nobody ever bares their breasts in front of the manager!" He nudges her gently in her side and adds, "Frank is a gentleman. We can go soon. The little one will be useful to us, you'll see."

***

"Pero, no conozco Roberto o Susan!" The nurse, who has been asked again, raises her shoulders, but has only eyes for Frank. "What about Simon Zimmermann? Do you know him?" Frank takes her hand, which makes her even more infatuated, and her eyes get very big at first, but then squeeze slowly down to small slits. She turns her head slowly towards Linda

225

and asks: "Who is that? His wife?" Then she releases her hand from Frank's, takes a menacing step towards Linda, grab's Linda's narrow waist with both hands, and hisses, "Are you Mirjam's mamá?"

Chapter 66

"I'd better get someone to clean this up. I'll be right back!" Ken strokes the more than embarrassed Rosalía one last time down her back and takes a few steps away from the bed She raises her head and looks at him. Just before he gets to the door, she breaks her silence, "No, please don't!"

Kenneth stops in surprise and turns around to her. "Please what?" As he speaks, he walks back to her. "Get someone or come back?" He looks at her with a friendly smile and puts his hands in his pockets. The resuscitated physiotherapist bites her lower lip and then answers: "Neither one! Please, stay!"

***

After they have folded up the dirty blanket in silence, Rosalía sits next to Ken on the bed and drinks water from the glass. The young lawyer breaks the silence. "Do you feel better? You scared the hell out of us down there!" Rosa asks him, "Us? I remember helping the Scottish Señorita who was looking for her friend..." Ken's smile interrupts her: "Scottish señorita? Linda? What makes you think she's Scottish?" He sits down on the edge of the bed and turns sideways towards her, and she does the same. "Who are you anyway?" asks Rosa because she is not only surprised that this dream man apparently knows her interviewee but has also taken care of her so nicely. But before he can answer her, she slaps her thigh and looks towards the door. "That's right! She asked about Simon!" She gets up without looking at Ken and puts the glass back on the side table.

"Do you know him well?" Conley Junior interrupts her newly started rush of thoughts and she looks horrified into his kind eyes. "You too?!" She sits down next to him on the bed again and stares at him.

"WHO ARE YOU???"

Chapter 67

"You know Mirjam? Where is she?" Linda doesn't hear the note of disapproval in the nurse's tone and also does not seem to notice her threatening posture. Frank intervenes elegantly in this feminine scene. "You must be Simon's girlfriend!" Carmelita looks at Frank in irritation. "Did he tell you about ME? Or the crazy cucaracha?!" Disapprovingly, she turns her head towards the fire escape.

"Crazy cucaracha?" Frank has question marks written all over his face as he asks this counter question.

"Yes, that crazy Rosalía! His boss, so to speak... She's always talking to herself and doing strange things here, so she is always being called in to the director general's office! Yes, her! She works in the Physiotherapy department and had something going on with Simon. Although she doesn't suit him at all... Crazy witch!" Linda interrupts her angry rant by placing her hand on her flat chest and gently saying, "I'm not Simon's wife. I just want to visit Mirjam. I am a friend from Switzerland and I haven't had a chance to see the little one. Do you know where she is?"

Frank and Tom look at each other in surprise. They hardly recognize Linda right now. She has started her chess game! One step after the other. They see in her sparkling eyes that the well thought out and focused battle plan has now been put into action.

"Sí, por supuesto qué sé! She's in the... Ah mierda, como se dice en ingles..." Carmelita flicks her long thin fingers into the air.

"Guardería, nursery, qué quieren decir?" Tom throws some suggestions out.

"Oh yeah! You speak Spanish! Sí, sí, Mirjam está en la guardería de esta clínica. Linda chica! Simon la trajo una vez..." The talkative colleague throws gossip at Tom as if they were old acquaintances. He smiles at her and asks," Donde está la guardería?"

She buttons up the top buttons of her smock and looks around the corridor. "I don't know if I can just tell you... Maybe it would be better if you first ask Simon? Does he know you're here?" She blinks her eyelashes at Frank again and adds, "He never told me he has such famous friends in America!" Frank winks at her mischievously. "Well, we all have our secrets, don't we? Unfortunately, we just missed Simon... But..."

"No, no, he is here! I just saw him with a patient... Un momento, mi amor!" She lifts her left index finger into the air as she takes a sort of cellphone out of her pocket.

Chapter 68

"I'm Kenneth Conley, a law professor from New York. My dad and I are accompanying a friend from Switzerland in search of her family, who we suspect is here in Mexico. I'm aware that sounds a bit strange, but it's the extremely short version of who I am..." He supports himself with his hand on the bed and leans forward to Rosalía, who simultaneously moves further away and covers her mouth with her hand, looking at him sadly. "From Switzerland? Dios... mio... Is she... Well..." She puts her hand on her thigh and looks at the door. Tears run silently down her cheeks and she swallows loudly before she goes on to say, "Her quest is over here..." She looks at her Highlander and adds, "The Director General does not yet know the connection... But I do... I know everything..."

"What do you mean, Rosalía? Can you help us? So you know Simon. Have I understood that correctly? Where is he?" The many questions come so quickly and excitedly in succession that Rosalía waves both of her hands and puts a finger on her mouth." Shhhh!!! Not so loud! This is a madhouse! And there's a witch hanging around out there who must NOT catch us! Do you understand?" She puts a hand on Ken's and looks at him seriously. "I am NOT crazy! Ok? Believe me, everything I tell you now is true, even if it sounds crazy! Ok? Do you trust me? Do you believe me? I'm not crazy!"

"Why should I think that? Of course you are not crazy!" He puts his other hand on hers and looks at her intently. He gazes at her beautiful face, her delicate nose, her full lips, her beautifully shaped cheekbones and then looks directly into her darkly sparkling eyes. She notices his scrutinizing look and her pulse artery begins to throb even more, as she gathers all her courage and tells the man of her dreams, who is sitting on the bed with her, the horror stories of the last few days.

Chapter 69

"Hola, amor!" Before the enchanted smiling Carmelita can continue speaking into the phone, Frank takes it casually out of her hand, presses the red button and puts his arm around her hips. "Oh, we don't want to spoil the surprise for Simon. He will be MUCH more pleased to know that his future señora has helped us. We men like such self-confident, self-assured and strong women! I very much hope he really appreciates what a pearl he has fished from the sea, Carmelita!" As he sends her flying to cloud nine with his words, he walks with her a bit down the corridor, away from the two listeners.

He knows this gesture will make her start gossiping again, so he whispers to her, "If you tell me where the nursery is, I promise to never tell your Simon that I've touched your lace bra!... He wouldn't like it much. He is a very jealous man, believe me, he can be very dangerous..." He winks at her and waits for her reaction.

***

Frank takes Carmelita's hand in his big hands, kisses the back of her hand, and performs a gentlemanly bow before he triumphantly returns to Linda and Tom. He gestures at them with two thumbs up and then points toward the fire escape. Tom briefly touches his arm and says, "And Ken? He's still in there!" His thumb points over his shoulder in the other direction down the corridor. Linda does not move at all, as if she has turned to stone.

"Linda! Come on! We're going to get Mirjam!" Conley looks at her in confusion. But when he sees the look in her eyes, he walks up to her, hugs her, kisses her on the head and whispers, "First the little one. We'll come back for Roberto! I promise! But first the little one!"

Chapter 70

Ken walks up and down the room like an absentminded professor, which he actually is right now.

"Let me get this straight! Bob... Well, Roberto is still alive! But Simon does not know that? At least that's what Roberto thinks... Do you know where this accident happened? On

Mexican or American soil? Did he just say the word 'border'?" He notices how brusque this questioning must appear to Rosalía and goes over to her: "Sorry, Rosa, that was not what I meant! I, I cannot imagine how difficult all of this must be for you! And then the thing with Simon! I just do not understand why you would spy on him... It cannot be only because of the fake documents... Or is it?... Blackmail?" He paces back and forth in the room and looks up at the ceiling. "That little piece of...!!! Of course it's blackmail! That would bring him a lot of money!" Ken notices a slight smile on Rosalías face as she looks ahead and he stops short in surprise.

"Lo siento mucho, Señor! But with everything here so terrible and unimaginable... I've never met a man who also talks to himself... A big, if not THE greatest weakness of mine...!" She blinks sheepishly and then stands there as if she's just made an important decision.

"But enough of this! We have better things to do now! Am I correct in assuming that calling the Policía would be the wrong tactic now?" She starts walking over to the door without waiting for his answer and looks back at Ken. "Nice to have met you, Señor Conley, if I don't get the opportunity to tell you that later. You may have yanked me out of my dream, but I now know that justice always wins in the end, and that gives me hope and I will not give up my dreams."

She waves the dumbfounded lawyer over to her and says seriously, "Come on, Professor of Law from New York, Rosalía now wants to know what's in this package!"

Chapter 71

The three visitors stop just in front of the somewhat secluded pavilion. "I think it's better to wait out here. One fan scene was enough for me today. And your Spanish is certainly more helpful here than my macho appearance." Frank puts his hand on Tom's shoulder and looks at Linda. "Come on, go get your daughter back! Bring Mirjam into our new family!"

"No, please come with me, Frank! I need you here!" For the first time since the two met, Linda is telling him that she needs him. These words go through Frank like an electric shower of sparks. His heart starts to flutter and his pulse beats stronger. A warm, comforting and almost tender feeling spreads throughout his body and he smiles a smile that neither Linda nor Tom have ever seen. He takes her outstretched hand and silently walks beside her to the bungalow door. Tom opens the old, brightly painted wooden door and lets Linda be the first go through.

***

"Bueños días, Señora. Puedo ayudarle?" Astonished at this strange visit, the elderly, small and plump Mexican woman looks at the three people. She holds her plump hands folded under her ample breasts and smiles kindly at them. Linda thinks of how happy children must feel in her care and is grateful that Mirjam is well looked after here. Rather, she WAS! Now Mirjam is coming home with her real family. With her mama.

Linda takes a step closer to the nanny and extends her hand in greeting. "Bueños días, Señora. Do you speak English?" The tiny woman does not answer her, just looks at her questioningly. Tom walks over to stand next to Linda, greets the Señora, and adds in Spanish, "We are friends of Simon Zimmermann. He has to work longer today and asked us to take Mirjam home. But I assume you already know that. He informed you about this, right, Señora Ramírez?" Linda looks at him in astonishment and Frank smiles at his clever agent as he sees photos of the employees, labeled with their names, hanging on the wall.

Chapter 72

She tentatively opens the door to the corridor and sticks her head through the crack. She listens and opens the door a little more. Rosalía feels the warm body of Ken standing behind her, feeling his breath on her neck and wishing this moment was not here and now, but on horseback in her dream. Softly Ken whispers in her ear, "Who are we afraid of?" Rosa chuckles just as softly and calls herself a fool for acting like a schoolgirl in love in the middle of this horrible story. Does he have to have such witty charm?

"The witch Carmelita! Simon's girlfriend!" She feels a jolt behind her and looks back. Ken looks at her in surprise. "He also has a girlfriend here?" Now it's the small Mexican woman's turn to have question marks written all over her face.

"Excuse me, what?" She puts both hands on her narrow waist and looks at the innocent professor angrily. "He has a girlfriend in New York? Well, it's very interesting to hear about everything this Simon still has to keep secret! Roberto also said nothing about this. So she doesn't seem to have been very important." She starts to turn away when Ken replies, "Well, I wouldn't say that. She was at least the key figure in the matter. She was the nurse who cared for Jasmine, Mirjam's mother, after my dad took her to the hospital." Rosa stops, closes the door, and slowly turns to face Ken.

"Wait. The nurse, you say? How long has she still been alive? Jasmine, I mean." The physiotherapist, crossing her arms over her chest, waits for Ken's answer, He wrinkles his forehead and supports himself with one hand on the closed door.

"I don't quite understand. What do you mean by how long she has she still been alive? Jasmine didn't die. She survived and is here in Mexico to get Mirjam. I told you that!" He points to the bed with his other hand, as if to remind her of the situation. "No, you didn't! I am confused now and then, and admittedly very often talk to myself! But I never forget what I've been told. I have an elephant brain! Yes, I do. Even though we don't have any elephants here in Mexico, well, we have some in the zoo, but not out in the wild... Rosalía, Dios mio, Rosa, get to the point!"

She throws both hands in the air and notices that her behavior seems to amuse the young lawyer. He smiles almost secretly and bends down to her. She can smell his breathtaking aftershave up close and remembers right at that moment her vomit on the bed!

"What exactly did I say?" His smiling eyes sparkle at her and she wants to tell him all the memories she has stored in her elephant-like brain, when there's a knock at the door.

Chapter 73

Because of her gestures and the fact that Señora Ramirez starts looking for something on the small desk, Linda and Frank look at each other. Linda moves closer to the action hero, wraps her arm around his as if she needs to hold herself upright with his help. He puts his large warm hand on her arm and kisses her on the forehead, whispering, "Don't worry, Tom will do it. If anybody can do it, it's that clever fox!" Linda nods, pressing her lips together and whispering anxiously, "And Susie, what about her?" She hardly dares to say that name and her eyes fill with tears. Conley turns to her and winks at her. "No, we definitely don't need to worry about Susie, Linda. I have a lot of faith in that powerful woman!"

"Linda?" Tom interrupts the couple's whispered conversation and extends his hand in her direction. "Would you like to wake the little girl herself or should the nanny go get her for you?"

The Swiss woman's face turns chalk white. Her cold hands are trembling, her mouth gets dry, her heart rate goes up quickly, and her legs appear to no longer be able to hold her upright. Frank initially gives her a happy look, but then notices her growing stiffness and puts his arm around her.

"We better wait here so the little girl doesn't get frightened...", he replies instead of Linda. He then addresses her., trying to lighten up the situation a bit. "It's been an eternity ago, but I still remember it very well. Ken never liked it if someone else woke him up instead of Heather or Bonnie."

He gives Tom a sign with his head that tells his agent to tell Señora Ramírez what their decision is. She agrees and as she leaves, she asks Tom something in Spanish. He looks first at Linda and then answers the question himself.

"What did she ask, Tom?" Linda's face seems to be recovering, but her ice-cold hands claw at Frank's arm.

Tom goes over to them, puts both his hands in his pockets and answers, "Whether she should immediately pack all of Mirjam's things because I told her that we are all taking a long vacation together." He smiles at Linda, while he steps back and forth from foot to foot. "And I told her 'yes'!"

Chapter 74

Rosalía opens the door and standing right in front of her is Carmelita, the last person she wants to encounter now. On second thought, she has to admit that there are more people on that list and she gives the nurse an overly friendly smile. "AWW... Carmelita! How nice of you to look out for me! I'm fine again! Thanks for asking! This young gentleman has been making sure that I don't do anything stupid here... Oh... I had to vomit... Lo siento mucho!... Should I take it to the laundry myself?" Hastily, like her ramblings, she walks past the surprised Ken and bends over the folded blanket. She hears Carmelita's loud gum chewing and knows she's busy assessing Ken.

"You definitely do not know each other yet!" As she walks back, Rosalia laughs embarrassingly loud and Ken frowns.

"Carmelita, this is a professor from New York. He apparently brought me here after I fainted. Señor Professor, this is our charming nurse Carmelita. Simon's girlfriend!" She gives her Highlander a meaningful look and squeezes between Carmelita and the door frame.

"You know Simon also? This seems to be my lucky day today! Look, cucaracha!" Carmelita seductively turns her gaze away from Ken, looks up at Rosalía with her eyebrow raised, and opens the top buttons of her skintight smock. "Carmelita, what are you doing?" Outraged, Rosalía starts to prevent further unbuttoning, but then the proud nurse shows off her trophy. The small physiotherapist doesn't know how she's supposed to react and raises her shoulders questioningly. "Frank Conley did this! You must know who Frank Conley is, cucaracha?!" She puts both of her hands on Rosa's narrow waist and looks at her in horror.

"Oh, you met Frank Conley? How exciting!" Ken joins the two women in the doorway with a mischievous grin and takes a quick look at the sexy face that Carmelita is still presenting freely, beaming at him. "Sí, are you American too?" After turning away from Rosalía, she now devotes her full attention to the young professor. "And are you also a friend of Simon's?" She leaves her smock open and extends her hand in greeting.

Take advantage of this moment, Rosa thinks to herself, and starts walking slowly down the corridor, still holding the blanket with the smelly contents in her hands.

Chapter 75

Frank's Blackberry starts vibrating intrusively in his trouser pocket, so that it also attracts the attention of the other two people waiting with him. "Don't you want to answer that?" Tom points to Conley's pants with his hand. "No, not now!" He raises both hands, as if in prayer, and again looks intently at the door, through which the tiny nanny has gone as if an eternity ago.

"And if it's Susie?" Startled, Linda looks into his familiar eyes, and he instantly shares the emotion. Conley hastily reaches into his pocket and looks at the screen of his phone. He just as quickly swipes his finger over it and holds it up to his ear: "Susie!? Where are you? Are you alright?"

He turns away and covers his other ear with his other hand. "I can barely hear you!! Where are you?!" Linda and Tom look at each other intently and try to find out more by running after Frank.

"He WHAT? But... How... For heaven's sake, Susie! I am so sorry! What, what does he want!?... Hello...?! Susie...?!... Ohh... Hello

Simon! What do you want? This is not an action movie, my man. Believe me, I know what I'm talking about!" Frank places a hand on his forehead as he looks out of the window in front of him. "Please, what is going on? They are just making everything a lot worse. We should think about Mirjam... And... And also about your future! Do you want to be on the run for life? We will find a solution! Tell me what you want, so that Susan Manders can come back to us!"

"Señorita?" A timid woman's voice yanks Linda out of this inexplicable situation and she looks behind her. Señora Ramírez is standing with a bag in her hand right behind her and she's holding it out to her. Pointing to Tom, she accompanies this action with Spanish words, which Tom simultaneously interprets. "These are Mirjam's things. Spare clothes, powdered milk and bottles. She doesn't like the pacifier, but you certainly know that. That's why you got rid of of it a long time ago. Valeria is still freshening Mirjam up. She had a full diaper. We will miss the sweet ray of sunshine very much. She has such a happy nature, considering that she has to grow up completely without Mamá. But I'm certain Simon has come up with a good plan for her. He is such a caring and loving father! In any case, we wish you a relaxing vacation and we look forward to having Mirjam back with us soon."

Chapter 76

Quietly, as if walking on clouds, the athletic physiotherapist scurries along the corridor and passes by the nurse's station. She arbitrarily opens a door and throws the crumpled, smelly blanket into the room. She closes the door almost silently and listens to see if she can still hear them talking. "Disgusting!" She speaks softly to herself. "You can hear her chewing gum popping all the way over here!" She rolls her eyes and pities Ken. "Well, what the heck. He survived my embarrassing self-talk and my vomit, so he can cope with this snake!" She throws her hand over her head and heads over to the next door. But before she can turn the doorknob, she looks back and feels a slight feeling... Yes, what was that...? Jealousy?

"You're crazy, Rosa! You don't want an American! And you do not even know him! A wonderful dream and beautiful eyes are not enough! So stop this! Leave it all to Carmelita! She devours one right after the other and shows her wondrous breasts to every single one of them!"

While she thinks about the fact that this is not the first time she has considered herself to be a fool in recent weeks, she enters unnoticed into the hospital room and closes the door behind her.

"Bob? Roberto?" Rosa whispers his name as if someone could hear her, and she walks cautiously toward the bed where her favorite patient is still motionless, his eyes closed and his chest moving very slowly up and down. She looks around the room but can't see the package anywhere. She carefully sits down on the edge of the bed, next to the sleeping man, and looks pitifully at the half-burned face, and gently strokes the scarred crust on one cheek and lets her index finger slide over the closed eyelid.

Her brain cannot respond to each influence at the same time. Because of this, her vocal cords remain mute, but her hand gives a defensive reflex and slaps the patient in the face. "Estàn girando?! Are you crazy?!" She jerks up and holds her violent hand to her chest, closing her eyes and taking a deep breath.

"I'm sorry, Rosalía! I am sorry! I... I didn't know if it was really you... Please, I'm sorry!"

Roberto reaches his hand out to her and smiles at her with his less injured eye.

"Yes exactly! Every woman here in this madhouse is talking to herself in my voice! They almost scared me to death! You madman! Where is the package?" In order to avoid wasting more precious time, Rosalía looks around the room again, but this time with more focus.

"Here! I hid it when you were talking to the psychiatrist and your best friend about the pills." He points his hand to his legs and Rosa throws the covers back off of his feet. She takes the carefully packaged box off the bed and sits down with it next to him.

"And the pills?" She opens her hand demonstratively in front of his face and he reaches with his hand under the covers. "I don't think you can still use them... Sorry..." Slowly his hand reappears and when he opens it, Rosa looks at a handful of pills.

Chapter 77

Linda silently takes the bag being held out to her and suppresses any resentment towards the nanny's ignorance. She gives Tom a meaningful look and he thanks the nanny also on behalf of Simon for the nice compliments. The nanny says a few sentences before turning and walking back through the door to the group of children. Linda looks at Tom. "Thank you, Tom! I have not said that yet, but I really appreciate what you do for me!" She points her finger and adds, "Even if you see it as your duty, or because you're being paid for it! I myself, Linda, thank you from the bottom of my heart!"

Tom takes the bag from her, slightly ashamed, and replies, "Thank you, Linda. That means a lot to me! I think it's better if I take this.

You'll need both hands!" They smile gratefully at each other and return their attention to Frank, who is still on the phone.

"Of course you can! What would be wrong with that?" Frank seems to be deep in the middle of a strategic negotiation and continues his concentrated conversation. "Put Mike on the phone!" His energetic tone scares Linda and she looks behind him to see if his phone call could be a disruption in this environment. Tom notices her worried look and leads the still talking Frank by his arm in the direction of the door. Frank is a bit confused about Tom's gesture and looks at Linda. He stops his manager and points his finger in the air, as if to say, "Wait a minute, I'm almost done!'

"Mike? Mike, wherever he wants to go, fly him there! Susan stays here! She MUST stay here!... Yes, of course Costa Rica! It doesn't matter where! Just take that man away from here!... What do you mean? Why would he do that?... Mike?!... MIKE!?" Perplexed, Frank looks at his Blackberry screen and frowns. He presses on it with both hands and starts to press the dial button when the door opens into the room and a petite, young woman holding a cloth with colorful embroidery on it and filled with something enters. All three of them stop breathing. No one moves, so the woman with the bundle in her arms goes straight over to Linda. Halfway there, the beautiful piece of cloth moves and the sound of a squealing baby can be heard.

Linda slaps her hands over her mouth and looks down at the moving bundle of bright Mexican colors with tear-filled eyes.

Chapter 78

Slowly, one tablet after the other drops into the trash can next to the bed and Rosalía counts loudly. "Caramba! They would have killed you if you had taken all this!" She swipes at his hand as a gesture to leave this behind.

"Bob, before we open this package, I have something to tell you..." She looks at him thoughtfully, then takes his hand again, which immediately closes around hers. "What is it, Rosa? What do you have to tell me or can it wait until we're outside?" Irritated, she looks into the injured eyes, which try to focus on her in the room.

"Outside? Where outside? I don't understand!" Roberto's hand still holds hers tightly and when he answers her, he takes her other hand in his other one, also enfolding it. "That's why you're here! To get me out of here, right? I thought that after I pretended to take the pills like a nice boy to calm down the Psycho, you would certainly dare to make the next move! No? What I have misunderstood?" His damaged eyes are still trying to catch her gaze, making him look so helpless that Rosalía's heart almost breaks.

"Oh, Bob! I haven't even had a chance to think about that! You have no idea what I have experienced in the past few hours... And you know what? It has EVERYTHING to do with you!"

She takes her hands out of his and taps her index finger on his chest, just enough for him to feel it. Roberto struggles to sit up in the bed and moans from the pain. "And that's good? At least you're not as mad at me as you were when we talked last time. What has changed?"

"The facts about what you and Simon did, even if you were only a means to an end, but my opinion of it all has not changed! I still think you're a cowardly monster! But... One thing has indeed changed... Even for you, my friend!"

"Now stop teasing me – it's torture! What is going on? What happened? Does it have anything to do with Simon? Is it something to do with Mirjam?" Rosa understands his almost exploding curiosity, mixed with panic, hope and fear. But she can't find the right words to form a sensible, informative sentence. She closes her eyes, takes a deep breath and starts to subconsciously give free rein to finally doing the right thing, when the door slowly opens.

***

OUTRODUCTION

"You did a great job, Querída!... Of course not!.... What makes you think that?... I would never think that! To me, you are the greatest nurse in the world!... No! You are absolutely right. To me, YOU are the greatest in the world... See you later then, just like we agreed?... Wonderful!... Té quiero!" Simon puts the phone in his pocket and looks into the scornful eyes of Susan Manders.

"Well, what can I say, I'm just crazy for little ones! It's a pity you will not meet her!" He raises his shoulders and immediately drops them again. "At least, it's obvious that she is more important to me than you are to the good Frank! Is anything going on between the old man and Jasmine? I could never stand that know-it-all woman professor... No idea what Roberto saw in her! Oh well, it's none of my business! We'll go get my little girl now and then we're off to Costa Rica! I need a vacation badly! This Rosalía really ran me off my feet... What a crazy woman!"

As he babbles on, he hands two bags to Mike, who places them carefully under the seat of his mobile workstation and looks at Susie questioningly. She raises a cool eyebrow and turns to Simon. "What does Leslie think of your new love?" Showing no emotion at all, Simon looks at Mike. "Ach, these women!" And to Susie, he says, "As far as I know, the nice lady cursed me out, didn't she? But that no longer matters. I have what I always wanted and that's Mirjam. And now we will go get her!"

"But Frank already did that! That's why I am no longer important to him in your eyes!" Susan lets Mike help her into the helicopter, but her gaze does not leave Simon's face. She does not want to miss a second of his expression, of the look on his face.

Simon grins mischievously, puts on the headphones and returns her gaze. "No, he didn't! He's taking care of a poor little orphan right now... Like I said, Carmelita is worth her weight in gold! And a Mexican family that sticks together should never be underestimated."

As Mike flies Frank Conley's helicopter to the mental hospital and its landing site, Susan Manders looks down on the Mexican landscape and thanks God for her two sons, whom she will never call idiots again. That is, if she ever sees them again.

***